VIA Folios 165

She's Not There

Original cover image by Joakim Berndes, CC BY-SA 4.0, via Wikimedia Commons.

Library of Congress Control Number: 2023940259

Published by
BORDIGHERA PRESS
John D. Calandra Italian American Institute
25 W. 43rd Street, 17th Floor
New York, NY 10036

VIA Folios 165
ISBN 978-1-59954-199-0

She's Not There

A novel by Richard Vetere

BORDIGHERA PRESS

"Well, let me tell you about the way she looked
the way she acts and the color of her hair
her voice was soft and cool, her eyes were clear and bright
but she's not there."

THE ZOMBIES 1965

1

In the summer of 1965, I had just turned thirteen and my mother ran away. I can't remember all the details of that summer but I do remember the broad strokes and they were that my mother had run away and my father sent me to live with his sister and her husband.

My aunt and uncle had a house in upstate New York and though my mother had disappeared without even leaving a note I wasn't too upset. My parents argued a lot and I thought it was something that they did all the time anyway and that my mother leaving was just one of those things married people did to one another.

Of course, that is what I thought since it was over fifty years ago that all this happened and looking back I can only say that I remember it all through the prism of someone much older than even my parents were at the time all this happened.

I shared the situation with my best friend Frankie and he shared with me that his own parents were constantly threatening to leave one another and he had even heard of a cousin who left his wife to be with another woman who, according to Frankie, was already married to his best friend.

So, thinking back, I saw getting out of the city for a few days might be a worthwhile adventure and I embraced it with open arms. However, I had no idea that I'd be spending the entire summer in a small place which seemed to me at the time to be the middle of nowhere.

It all started when I came home from my last day of school before the summer break and my mother wasn't home. She was always home waiting for me so it was odd not to see her waiting for me. We lived in a nice brick house in Maspeth, Queens near the park and not far from Shea Stadium. I loved the Mets but I loved the LA Dodgers even more mainly because I loved Sandy Koufax. He was the best pitcher in baseball and I loved the blue and white uniforms the Dodgers wore.

It was always quiet and residential in my neighborhood all year long. I even noticed that our car, a white Ford Fairlane, was not parked in front of our house.

I didn't think anything of it, so I rushed out to play with my friends down the park. However, when I did get home for dinner there was a police car parked in front of the Ford Fairlane. When I went inside my father was in the living room looking distraught though happy to see me. There were two uniformed police officers standing with him.

"You're here," my father stated.

"Sure, Pop, why wouldn't I be?"

That's when one of the cops spoke up. "She's an adult, Mister Ricci, and adults can come and go as they please if they are married or not. This happens more than you think. A spouse goes for a pack of cigarettes and they don't come home." Then the other smaller cop added, "Sometimes for weeks and sometimes never."

"We got all her information," the first cop said.

"She'll show up in no time," the second cop told my father and then both cops walked out of the house.

My father sat down on the sofa and lowered his head. He then quickly looked up at me as if he realized that me, seeing him that troubled, might worry me.

"Mom smokes?" I asked. "I didn't know she smoked."

"She didn't want you to see her smoke."

"How come?"

He was puzzled by my question but then opened up. "Look, Chris, your mother and I had a fight. I put some money down on the Yankees and they lost. She was angry with me."

"Yeah, I heard they lost again."

"It was a lot of money that I lost. So, she ran away."

"Ran away?"

"Yes."

"I thought only kids run away."

"Well, it's not the same. Kids run away but they have to come home again. With adults it's different."

"How different?"

"Well, adults don't have to come home. I mean, they do come home but there's no law to say that they have to come home. Like it is with kids."

"That's weird."

"Did she say anything to you this morning before you went to school?"

"About what?"

He lowered his head again. He shrugged. "I have a feeling she went to her sisters out in Pennsylvania. I see that the food money is gone from the container in the top drawer."

I knew about the food money they kept in a big plaster beige pig my father always called the container.

"She's coming back, right?" I asked.

He stood up and went over to me. He didn't exactly hug me, but I do recall that he got really close to doing it. "Yeah, she's coming back. She's just letting off steam."

"Oh."

"But I have to give her some room. You know, breathing room to get over being mad at me."

I always remember my father having big warm dark eyes. He had wavy black hair cut neatly for his job. He was a clerk and worked for a big company that did inventory in Manhattan.

I don't remember much more from that night, but I do remember that when eventually I went to bed, I was feeling a little upset that my mother would run away without saying goodbye to me. I also couldn't figure how she could leave me but then again, I was all of thirteen and I was certainly able to take care of myself, so I forgave her. However, the thought of living in Pennsylvania didn't appeal to me.

The next morning before the sun was even up my father was on the phone talking to my Aunt Angie telling her that he was putting me on a bus before he went to work.

"Don't forget to get him at the bus depot, Angie," I remember him telling her on the phone.

I thought it was strange that he had to remind her. How do you forget to pick up a kid? I thought all adults were in my life to make sure they took care of me. I was learning that that wasn't always the case and it through me off balance.

My father helped me pack all my summer clothes in one suitcase. I took a few books that I wanted to have with me, my toothbrush, my ten-cent comb, my new brown leather wristband and my song book. I wanted desperately to learn how to play the guitar that summer but before I dared attempt it, I bought a song book hoping to teach myself how to learn to read music and play cords.

I also took with me my baseball cards. My favorite were of Bob Gibson, Mickey Mantle, Gil Hodges and of course Sandy Koufax.

I also took along my transistor radio. My favorite group was the Four Seasons and the very first song I ever heard was "Sherry." I was in the back seat of my car when it played on the radio. My mother and father were in the front seat, and we were coming home from somewhere.

We were just exiting the Long Island Expressway exit ramp at Maurice Avenue when it came on the radio. I was ten or eleven when I heard it. It was so strange to hear a song that suddenly made you think about yourself. I had never really thought about myself as a boy who might have feelings for a girl but hearing that song made me think it was something that might happen to me.

It was also that summer, or the summer before, that I became more aware of the routine of life. I liked routine and the routine was that I went to school all winter and I was allowed to stay home all summer.

My mother stopped working part-time. She was a waitress in Williamsburg, Brooklyn where she grew up and now, that I was home from school, she also stayed home to babysit me.

I used to play alone in the alleyway behind my house. My favorite game was being a U.S. Marshal in the Wild West and it was my job to find the bad guys and bring them to justice. I would walk the alleyway with a fake six gun on my belt, a white cowboy hat and sneakers looking for trouble. I can still see the bright sunshine spreading across the alleyway's concrete floor, edging down through the two-story brick buildings as I sauntered through the imaginary town.

Those mornings were so quiet and peaceful I could hear myself think. I would talk to myself telling myself that I was ready and able to tame any lawlessness when I had to. I also felt like I was growing as a boy and slowly into a man though I was just a teenager back then. I can hear my mother talk to her neighbors in the kitchen about how I played cowboy. Looking back, I realize now she talked about me with a lot of pride. She would make lunch for me, and I would eat it in the kitchen at the table looking out into the sunshine and Mount Zion Cemetery out in the distance and the Manhattan skyline beyond it.

That was about all I could remember from those days other than when my father took a vacation. He always got two weeks and he always took them in August.

The first week of our vacation we would eat out every night. My mother was never much of a cook so going out to dinner was a major treat for me.

Monday night my father would take us to the diner in Long Island City at Hunters Point. I remember having onion soup and the delicious small brown roles I had never seen before. It was processed and full of sugar but I really enjoyed it.

Tuesday night we went to an Italian restaurant in Williamsburg, and I loved the food. I always had pasta and meatballs. Wednesday, we went to the Sage Diner on Queens Boulevard where I had chicken soup and omelets with French fries. Thursday, we went to White Castles for burgers and Friday night was the night my father ordered take-out Chinese food. And my mother allowed me to drink soda since at home all we were allowed was milk. I don't think we ever drank water. My favorite soda was Coke-Cola, and I drank as much as I was allowed.

The second week of my father's vacation we went to a summer resort in Lake George, New York. I have fond memories of morning breakfast looking at the squirrels racing around outside the window while I enjoyed my pancakes. But now, with my mother gone, all of my routine was going to disappear.

*

My father then drove me down to Port Authority in midtown, bought me a bus ticket, and the next thing I knew I was looking back at him out the window before he raced away to his car before he got a parking ticket.

The empty bus quickly headed north. With the sun rising over New Jersey and the Hudson River, I knew I was headed north. I struggled with the reality that I wasn't sure when I was going to see my best friend Frankie, my father and my mother again.

All along the bus ride I thought of how I always wanted to travel the country in a Ford Mustang. I had watched a TV show called *Route 66* where these two guys drove a hot Corvette around the country. I wanted to hop in a car like that, speed across the country with my best friends or even my best girl.

I had no idea what to speed across the country meant. All I knew of the country was New York City and now I was going to find out a lot more about Upstate New York.

*

My aunt and uncle lived in the middle of nowhere in a small village named Old Bridge outside a place named Saugerties. Looking back now I figured that my father sent me to stay with them for two reasons. He knew he couldn't work and at the same time watch over me and he wanted to place me away from the drama that may unfold.

I can't recall what I was thinking as the bus took me along the New York State Thruway which was Interstate 87 and left me off at the bus depot in Saugerties. I was the only person who disembarked and after the bus pulled away I was all alone with my suitcase.

I remember feeling a bit dizzy getting off that bus. It might have been the country air, the unknown world around me or the uncertainty of what was coming, but the dizziness didn't last long. My father told me that my aunt would meet me there, and even though I didn't recall what she looked like, there was no one there to meet me. I found a bench and sat down staring across the main street watching the occasional car pass and the handful of pedestrians who walked by.

Sitting on the bench I noticed how yellow everything was. Not used to being in the country I wasn't aware of how much sunlight there was in the world. From my perspective everything looked as if it had been dipped in yellow. Even the blue sky and the green in the trees and grassy fields had an impressive tint of yellow in them.

For a young boy who was used to jump starting his body to get to the school bus on time the luxury of just sitting on the bench allowing the morning to wash over me was a distinct pleasure I hadn't experienced before.

I don't remember how long I waited but ultimately a feeling of aloneness overcame me. I felt alone in the world for the first time in my young life. When I realized I didn't know anyone in my immediate vicinity, I was truly out of my element and the fact that my father was distraught and my mother had run away, made me feel like a solitary drifter. I looked around me and felt like I was an orphan or someone time forgot. I wondered if adults had these feelings as well.

Eventually an old dark green Dodge pulled up to the bus station. A woman with a mass of premature gray hair rolling around on her head peeked her face out of the car. "Christopher?" she asked.

I stood.

She opened the large door and got out of the car. She was tilting as she walked over to me. She was wearing a pale blue housedress and old worn brown shoes.

She leaned down and hugged me. I smelled the alcohol emanating from her as she did. I knew the smell from my father when he had a party with his friends. My father let me taste a drop of wine one night at one of those parties and I remembered not liking it.

"I had the wrong time!" She smiled then cheerfully picked up my suitcase, placed it in the back seat and then got behind the wheel.

I still hadn't moved.

"What's wrong?" she asked.

I murmured. "Should you drive?"

Perplexed, she frowned. "Oh, I can see fine enough without my glasses. How did you know I left them home?"

Not wanting to make more of a scene I got into the car and off she drove.

My aunt chatted away as she looked over the enormous dashboard and I looked up delighted at the rays of light that blasted down from the sky, through the trees and onto my face.

"Me and Marty are gonna take care of you. Your mother will show up soon enough but while you're here you will have a good old-fashioned summer."

I had no idea what a good old-fashioned summer was but with the window open I allowed the wind to caress my face as if I were on a magic carpet ride. It was fun seeing the hills off to my right and the large puffy white clouds to my left while my aunt drove us down the country road. It was a long ride through the hills passed stretches of cornfields and isolated farms dotting the landscape. On the last leg of our trip, I watched how my aunt barely navigated the curves on the single lane road all the while puffing on a cigarette that was dangling from her mouth. I didn't take too many glances at her since I didn't want to distract her and, to my delight, she was quiet until she reached her arm across my face pointing to a house off in the distance.

"There's the house!" she said and I looked. I saw a speck on a hill off in the distance on the other side of a large expansive field of grass and weeds. My aunt then followed the road around a long winding right turn and, just as we came out of the turn, we were under a canopy of massive, tall trees that entirely blocked the sun and it was completely gone. We drove out from the canopy and rays of light filtered through the large tree limbs splattering speckled rays down on us.

We soon reached a crossroads and my aunt turned right again this time going up a steep dirt road that rose again into the trees. I held onto the door handle as the car rocked, bouncing us both up and down as we drove over small sticks and branches.

"We had such a rain last night!" my aunt told me. Her voice was hoarse, and though she was a little older than my father, she sounded like someone's grandmother with the lilt of a frog in her voice.

We came down as quickly as we rose. The steep hill, and another right curve, took us passed a large barn. As we drove closer, I could see that the barn was rotting away. A tree had crashed into it. There was a gaping hole in its entire right side. It was so long ago that the tree and barn, both the same color gray, looked fused together.

"You remember the mushroom barn?"

My recollections of the barn were slight if anything. Before I had left my father reminded me that the last time I had been to my Aunt Angie and Uncle Marty's house, I was only five years old. My memories were of a summer long ago and my mother and father desperately trying to sleep in the oppressively humid, mountain air. Odd memories of a place I had only been to once before.

Once we drove passed the barn we drove to a small bridge that took us across a creek and then up another short hill. That's when I saw it standing in all its aging glory: the house.

I hadn't officially seen the movie *Psycho* since my father wouldn't allow it, but I did see the movie posters and my aunt and uncle's house looked exactly like the one standing on a hill, not entirely decrepit, but certainly haunted. Even in the bright sunlight it resembled the two-story gray wood and brick structure of the house in the movie with lone windows on the top floor peering eerily into the isolation surrounding it.

My aunt parked in the back of the house, which oddly faced the road, and when she opened the door, I heard dogs barking. One large mean looking black and white dog showed me his teeth as soon as he saw me. Satisfied that it scared the hell out of me, it quickly went back to a well-chewed bone. The dog was tied to an enormous gray tree. It was the biggest tree I ever saw.

"Shut up, Stalin," my aunt shouted back at the dog as two others came running to her looking to be greeted and petted.

"Stalin's bark is worse that his bite," she told me. She then greeted the two other dogs. "We got Pinky and Brownie," she said petting them.

Both were sleek, brown Shepard's turning to me for acknowledgement, as they checked me out to make sure I was a friend. I couldn't take my eyes off Stalin. "Do you ever let him run free?"

"Sometimes but only if we are watching him. He's part Russian mongrel that one. If we let him go he might run back to Moscow."

I had no idea if she was serious or not.

"It's kind of funny that we hate the Russians, but we love our Stalin."

"Ok," I replied.

"I have some lunch for you, Chris," my aunt then said, carrying my suitcase as she led me into the house.

To enter the house, you had to walk around to an enclosed porch. A thin wooden, squeaky door was part of the porch and once you entered the porch area, which was enclosed by a screen door, you would face the front door. The porch faced a cornfield and the one road beyond which we had just driven over. Once inside the house I had a flashback to the first time I had ever been inside. It was caused by the smell of mildew or mold that permeated the house like the odor of booze permeated the car.

The porch consisted of a long wooden table and flies. There were flies everywhere. There were dozens already dead having been caught on the overhanging fly strips. Once passed the porch and into the house, I came face to face with large stairs made of dark wood which led to the bedrooms on the second floor.

To the right was a dark living room and furniture that not only looked old but was made of dark wood and pine to make the room seem even darker. To the left, where my aunt led me, was the kitchen and beyond the kitchen a door leading to the basement.

"Get settled in!" she said with a big smile. "Your bedroom is the first door on the right at the top of the stairs." She then quickly poured herself a drink of what I would later learn was rye and soda and preceded to unwrap a sandwich for me. I quickly dragged my suitcase up the stairs reaching the top, out of breath. I found the first door to the right and opened it.

My bedroom looked much better than the rest of the house. I could see the bed was made with light green bed sheets and there was a desk and a large window which looked off to the large hill looming diagonally to the cornfield to the side of the house.

I opened my suitcase placing some of my clothes in the drawers and then went downstairs to the kitchen. My aunt was already gone but she left my ham and cheese sandwich and glass of milk for me which I ate heartily.

Once again, I found myself alone taken aback at how quiet the house was. The kitchen was small with lacey curtains on the windows and a large sink and refrigerator taking up most of the space. The table I sat at was surrounded by light blue metal chairs.

Sitting there I realized that I didn't hear any noise other than the occasional dog bark. There were no sounds of car traffic or overhead jets flying off to places I didn't think I'd ever see. I didn't even hear any birds singing either. All I did hear was the sound of the wind through the trees and my own thoughts racing through my head.

I was struck by the notion that I was going to spend an entire summer in these surroundings and for the first time I was terribly angry with my mother.

2

"So, you made it!" my Uncle Marty's said to me with his baritone voice stating a fact and not asking a question as he returned from work. He was a big man. He was tall and round with a large belly. He had long, thin spaghetti-like white hair strung across his large, bald head. He had a round face and small light blue eyes. Oddly enough he also had small hands. He walked quickly from his car to Stalin all the while gleefully focused on the dog.

I stood behind him having spent the day in my room looking out the window trying my best to get acclimated to my surroundings. I even took a nap on my bed finding the mattress to my liking. I also learned that there wasn't a bathroom in the house. They had an outhouse. My aunt showed it to me. It was a small wooden shack behind the large tree where Stalin was tied.

When showing me my room and explaining about the outhouse my aunt gestured to a small blue bowl on the table near my bed. "If you must take a piss in the middle of the night piss in that. You can pour it out on the grass in the back once you get up in the morning. If you must do number two then go to the outhouse. It ain't winter anymore so you won't freeze your tokus."

I met my uncle outside seeing his car drive down the road off in the distance then trying to time how long it would take to reach the house. He drove up in a large white pickup truck heaving his bulky frame out of the truck's cabin then, like I said, rushing over to Stalin hugging the dog as soon as he reached him. I thought that he greeted the animal with more affection that he did my aunt. He didn't even acknowledge her until he turned to her as she stood in the fading sunlight at the front door near the porch on the slight incline of grass. I saw her smiling at him with a twinkle in her eyes as if he were a little boy home from a day at school. He walked up the rise of the hill giving her a peck on the cheek when he reached her and then he turned to me.

"Look at you! You got so big!" he said as if seeing me for the first time. He nearly growled with delight but then quickly shouted at my aunt about her being late with dinner. He then tussled the hair on my head and led me into the kitchen. "He looks so big, Mama," he said.

I soon learned that my aunt and uncle called one another *Mama* and *Papa* for some reason that alluded me.

I sat quietly through dinner of pork chops and potatoes listening to my uncle talk about *the plant* which I eventually figured out was where he ran a large machine that made concrete. I watched as my aunt listened nonchalantly to the office politics as if she had heard it all before but wanted him to think that it was still important to her. My uncle drank a beer from the bottle but frowned when my aunt made herself a second *highball* of rye and soda.

"Another one, Mama?" he said but she ignored him.

At one point during dinner my uncle looked at the bottle standing in the corner on the counter away from the table. "That was barely touched when I left this morning," he said sharply.

"You got the wrong morning, Papa. That was yesterday. It's an old bottle and I hardly touched it all afternoon," she lied.

She looked at me. "After a while you can't tell one day from another out here. Except Saturday and Sunday."

My Uncle Marty devoured his dinner and talked while he ate. "Did your brother hear from her yet?" he asked.

"Nothing yet, Papa," my aunt replied.

"Not like her to go gallivanting around," he said. "But women have all these new ideas today with that feminism stuff. It makes them simply crazy with confusion. This thing about expressing themselves and such nonsense." He shook his head clearly editing himself with me in the room. He sat back down and sat back and grinned at me. "You want to see my rifles?"

After dinner I found myself in his den. I excitedly watched him open the lock to the glass closet where he kept his rifles. He pulled one out of the half-a-dozen weapons he kept on the wall. I specifically liked the doubled-gaged shotgun, and it was clear by his own glee that he enjoyed my excitement.

"I keep it loaded at all times," he told me.

We didn't talk much after that since, once he put the rifles away, he sat back in his big chair and put on the television. His TV set was small. Its screen was nothing more than a spec it was so tiny.

"You like *Bonanza*?"

"I do."

"I love that big Hoss," he said. "Great show."

As soon as its theme song played, he was dead asleep. He had the shotgun across his lap, and though he was sitting up, his chin was on his chest.

I wasn't exactly sure what to do. I didn't want to be in the room if the shotgun went off so I just left the room. I found my aunt sitting on the porch playing solitaire while heartily pouring herself another highball.

"He's out like a light I bet," she said to me.

"He is."

"He's up before the sun is, and he's out the door before I can even rollover," she told me. "That man works hard. You know we get to live in this house rent free thanks to his job. He's got a promotion coming up too. Is *Bonanza* still on?"

"It is."

She nodded then got up and I followed her into the den. She shut off the TV and put on the radio. Music played softly.

"He likes to watch *Bonanza* to put him to sleep but he likes nice music to sleep to once he's out," she said. "Complicated man he is."

"*Que sera sera/whatever will be will be*," played on the station. Doris Day sang the song.

My aunt then walked me back to the porch. The wooden floors creaking all the way there.

"You and I can watch *I Love Lucy* if you want?"

Though the den was dark the sun was still out since it was barely sunset this time of year. My aunt read my mind when I glanced at the porch door.

"You want to be with young folks your own age, I imagine."

I nodded.

"Not much to do out here though for a city boy," she said focused on her cards and her drink. "But you can go for a walk if you want. There's a house on the other side of the cornfield. They've got a young girl your age living there. The Viola's. Nice folks. Her name is Sarah. Take a walk over and introduce yourself."

I opened the door and stepped outside.

"When you walk back in the dark just follow the lights from the porch," she said through the screen windows.

I didn't get too far when I looked back. I could see my aunt in the porch light sitting alone sipping her highball by herself and right above her was the canopy of stars looking steadfast but as alone as she was.

*

I slowly entered the cornfield enthralled by the tall stalks of corn on either side of me and quickly disappeared into its world. The corn was standing in rows, and I found a path to walk through. It was made of light brown earth and the corn stood up on small mounds with each stalk's roots buried in the mound.

The more I walked the more I felt like an astronaut investigating a foreign planet. The tall stalks cut off all sounds and sights around me so all I knew was the world of the cornfield and what was right in front of me.

The setting sun made the green stalks and yellow buds of corn lifelike. They were standing straight up with their arms out, their heads facing forward, like alien beings. The deeper I walked into the cornfield the eerier the feeling.

The field stretched halfway to the road. It had to be two football fields long.

When the cornfield ended I found myself in a swirl of grass and weed stretching the rest of the way. There was only one house as far as I could see in any direction other than my aunt and uncles' and that was the Viola house.

I walked through the grass, weed fields, and saw that the house was on the side of a hill filled with trees. It was a two-story house not much different than my aunt and uncles'. It was made of wood and had a porch. There was a pickup truck parked near the front door and I saw a woman standing in the front yard taking clothes off a clothesline.

I walked towards her, and she quickly noticed me. She had on a housedress like my aunt wore and, like my aunt, she looked tired and plain.

She smiled at me when I got closer. "You're Angie's nephew, am I right?" she asked as she placed clothing in a wooden basket.

"I am," I answered. "My name's Chris," I told her.

"Well, Chris, did you come by to say hello to my daughter Sarah? I hear you might be here for the summer."

"I hope not that long," I said quickly.

"Well Sarah is at the Community Center. The kids go there at night." She pointed away from the setting sun. "It's only about a half a mile down the road. It's not much more than an old community center that only the kids use as a hang out now. Go down there and introduce yourself."

So, with that I headed down the road.

"Just tell my daughter not to stay out too late or I will come looking for her," I heard her shout to me as I headed away from the setting sun.

3

I heard the community center before I even reached it. The Rolling Stones song "*I Can't Get No Satisfaction*" was playing on somebody's transistor radio.

It was so quiet the rock and roll music resonated through the trees and the night air giving an invisible electricity to a place that had none of its own.

When I finally reached the center, the sun had set and a few road lamps lit the night. Swarms of moths buzzed around the lights flying around in frantic motions.

The center was nothing more than a run-down pile of wood with a small stage and a large canopy with a hole in the middle of it. I quickly figured it was the closest place for anyone to hang out other than in the woods if you couldn't drive and that's why the kids hung out there.

I walked through the doorway that didn't have a door and saw a pretty teenager sitting on what was left of a bench with an older teen who was smoking a cigarette.

The teen smoking a cigarette ignored me, but the other girl didn't. She smiled and I smiled back. Then she waved me over and I went to the bench.

There were three boys hanging out together on the far side of what was once a room, but they did nothing more than shoot me a glance.

They were huddled around the transistor radio like the moths were huddled around the lamp light. They were all skinny, young and in shorts.

"You're from the city," the younger pretty girl said to me getting my attention.

"I am," I answered not wanting to sound like a nerd by asking her how she knew.

"You walk like you're from the city," she said as if reading my mind.

Her soft light brown eyes had a spark in them that gave away her intelligence and curiosity in one glance. Her smile was not silly. It was heartfelt. It seemed that when she smiled, she meant it. I'd eventually learn that she didn't smile a lot and she didn't grace everyone with that smile.

I took a chance and asked. "Are you Sarah?"

She nodded with a slight sense of suspicion.

I told her what her mother had just told me about her not staying out too late and she immediately got up and walked away. I watched her rush down the few steps to the front of the center and stop. She turned to me.

"Already my mother is telling *you*, a complete stranger, what *I* should do?"

"I didn't mean anything by it. This is my first day here."

"I ain't blamin' you," she told me.

I nodded okay.

She looked away from me but then said, "You want to walk?"

"Sure," I said, and we left the others and their music behind.

"Where are you goin' Sarah?" the older teen asked. I learned eventually that her name was Marsha.

"I have to get home," Sarah shouted back.

"Mama's girl."

"You wish."

"Okay, leave me, see what I care," Marsha said as she turned to the others still hanging out.

We walked down the road into the hum of all kinds of flying and crawling bugs. Neither one of us said much but in a few moments I answered her inquiries about why I was *not* in the city for the summer and when I told her my mother had disappeared she asked. "Did that make you feel sad?"

"I don't think so. Not yet anyway."

"I'd like to do that, too, some day."

"You'd like to disappear?"

"Hell yes."

"Oh, you'd like to run away." I said.

"Oh yeah. Hey, what was it like being in the city when the blackout came?"

"I was home with my parents. I was really looking forward to seeing *Combat!* on TV that night. It was strange since all the lights outside went out. My father wouldn't let me go out, so we went to the roof instead. It was a bright, full moon with no clouds. It was so eerie. I mean, we could see the city skyline from our windows in the house in the back. Seeing the Empire State Building looking so dark was like seeing a dead guy standing up. And seeing the rest of the tall skyscrapers was like looking at a row of tombstones."

"Wow."

"What was it like up here?"

"Just another dark night."

She told me that she had only been to Brooklyn once, Queens never and Manhattan for one long summer afternoon and that was the extent of her travels.

She hated school, didn't like too many of her friends up in Old Bridge and wished she got to spend more time in Saugerties. That was the big city to her.

"Where's the old bridge your town is named after?"

"We don't have a bridge. Not any bridge. Not even an old one. Nobody knows why we're called Old Bridge. You ever hear of something so stupid. This whole place is stupid. You could call it dark side of the moon and it would still fit the place."

"Maybe there was a bridge here once," I said.

"We don't even have a river to put a bridge over."

As we walked, I took a closer look at her. She was slight with shoulder-length brown hair and a tight fitting dark green T-shirt and dark blue jeans. She wore bright white sneakers and had printed her name on both toes.

"Do you believe in the moon?" she asked me.

I looked up but I couldn't find it.

"It's behind the hill right now. But you don't have to see it to believe in it."

"*How* do you believe in the moon?"

She walked with tiny but confident steps. I saw she had a slight limp favoring her left leg.

"It's special. It's up there for all people on earth to see but nobody's been there. So, it's something you have to believe in to believe it's there. Some days and nights it's there and others it's not. It's special."

I wanted to understand her. I wasn't sure what she was trying to say but I liked it anyway.

"You saw that I limp."

"Yes."

"I was born with my left leg just like half an inch shorter than the right one. It's okay for now but the doctors said that if I grow to be six feet tall, I will be in trouble. Ha, I don't see that happening."

As we walked, I noticed that out in the country night had no sound other than crickets and sometimes the screech from an owl, or a dog's bark from off in the distance or the scary cry from a cat.

Sarah seemed one with the night easing through it in and out of shadow and light without missing a beat.

"I start high school in the fall," I told her.

"I don't want to go to high school. I want to travel. See things," she replied.

I found out that her father had left them only because her mother was a bitch and now he lived in Pennsylvania, and she lived with her mother and stepfather who she didn't like.

"My father is the best. Everything in my life that is good is because of him," she said.

When she talked about her father her eyes got wide and her voice went up. She told me how he had a decent job for the city of Scranton though she didn't exactly know what he did.

She also told me that he was handsome and tall and he never should had married her mother though if he hadn't she wouldn't have been born. "I guess you have to take the good with the bad."

She went on to tell me that her father told her that she could be anything she wanted to be and that in life she had to make herself happy first and everybody else was second.

"He looks like John Wayne. He really does. He's tall, and he walks like a real man. He doesn't talk a lot, but when he does, he says something, you know what I mean? And he's tough but not mean."

She also told me that the girl she was sitting with was named Marsha and she was a local too and Sarah only hung out with her since there weren't many other girls up in Old Bridge her age.

She told me that three boys I saw at the community center were cousins and they weren't very bright but they were *good kids*.

When we reached the cornfield I realize her house was directly to the right and mine was straight ahead. I didn't want to stop talking to her and I was relieved when she asked me if I wanted to sit on her porch.

We walked to her house and sat under the overhead light. It was warm enough that the windows to the house were open and I could hear a television set playing and a male voice asking for a beer.

"He's too lazy and too fat to get up and get anything for himself. Just because he pays the bills, he thinks the world owes him."

We sat side by side and I struggled to find something interesting to say. Everything she said to me sounded mature, fascinating, and honest. I hadn't ever spoken to anyone like her before.

At one time during the silence between us she took my hand. She held it but I wasn't sure why. She smoothed her fingers over my knuckles and then looked out into the darkness.

"You can tell a lot about people just from their hands," she said. "My father told me that once and it's true."

I wanted to reach out and touch her hands, but I was too shy. Instead, I nodded in agreement and matched her silence with my own.

"Just think about it," I said out of nowhere. "There's a big city somewhere with bright neon lights and millions of people having a big party right now!"

Sarah gave me her big candid smile. "Unbelievable, right?" I asked.

"Yes, it is! I mean, here we are looking out at all this dark. I mean nothing but bugs, mice, and trees but there's a whole world out there for us."

"I had a pretty interesting thought, right?"

She gave me her big smile again. "You did, Christopher, you did."

"Not too many people called me Christopher. My mother did occasionally but that was the only person who did. Everybody else calls me Chris. My best friend Frankie does."

Right then the screen door opened and like a bolt Sarah jumped up and rushed away. I quickly followed her.

When we got to the edge of the light she turned and pointed to the second-floor darkened window on the left.

"That's my bedroom."

When I turned to look, I saw her mother standing in the doorway.

"Sarah? What are you still doing out?" she shouted.

I could see Sarah cringe. "I better go. She can really throw a fit."

"Okay," I said.

With that she gave me a look. "See you tomorrow?"

"Yeah," I answered. "Oh, one day I am going to buy a red mustang and drive across the country. Will you come with me?"

She nodded enthusiastically. "Yes!" she answered. "Oh, do you know how to get home?"

"That's my aunt's house," I said pointing to the light off in the distance.

"Right. Oh, and don't get scared by the scarecrow. It looks so scary from my bedroom window," she told me with the slight sound of glee in her voice. With that she turned and ran to her front door.

I could hear her mother and stepfather say something to her as she entered the house and then the door slammed shut.

I was all alone. I looked up and saw a million stars and I felt even more alone.

I turned and headed into the cornfield. It was scary walking under the large stalks. In the darkness they looked like people leaning over and watching me.

Once I was in a few yards I ran. I couldn't help myself. I felt a tingling up my spine as if pursued by demons. I pushed my way through the shadows and just as Sarah warned I saw the scarecrow.

It was to my right several rows away. I could see it only because it was larger than the stalks of corn and hung over the entire cornfield like a huge bird. Seeing it made me run even faster kicking up the hard dirt with my sneakers as I did.

I didn't stop until I reached the small hill. I then rushed out of the cornfield and right up to the porch. Sweating and panting I stopped in my tracks when I saw my aunt.

Aunt Angie was slumped over the table under the bright porch light. I hesitated to go into the house but found the courage and opened the door.

I held the screen door so it wouldn't make any noise when it closed. I stood there looking at my aunt. She was leaning over the table with one hand clutching her deck of cards and the other on the table next to her drink. I surmised that she fell asleep right in the middle of a hand of solitaire. Her face was on her chest and her eyes were closed. The only sound I heard was of flies manically buzzing around right before they caught in the sticky fly catcher tape hanging from the ceiling.

I eased past my aunt into the kitchen and I could hear that the radio was still playing. I didn't want to wake her and thought it was best if I just let her sleep.

I then walked into the den and found my Uncle Marty in the same position he was in when I left him. He was snoring loudly in the dim lamp light with the double gauge shotgun in his lap.

I walked up the creaky stairs and into my room. Once inside I closed the door and sat on the bed. Just then the moon seemed to rise in the night sky outside my window. It seemed to bloom out of the night sky white and flat. It looked special.

I fell asleep thinking of Sarah and my fantasy red Mustang.

4

All that week I spent time together at the community center at night with Sarah. I got to know the other kids as well. Marsha was quiet and when she did speak, she always said something about someone focusing on their problems. She'd say something like "Sarah's biggest problem is that she's too nice to people." Or she'd talk about the cousins saying stuff like, "Jimmy's problem is that he doesn't know when to be quiet."

The people she thought had the biggest problems were her own parents and her older brother. According to *her*, her parents' problem was that they always wanted what everyone else had.

They wanted a bigger pickup or a bigger house or a better job than they had. She also thought her brother's problem was that he liked some girl in Woodstock named Candy who thought she was pretty, but she looked like a dog's ass.

I thought Marsha had a big problem and that was that nothing made her happy. I tried to imagine what life was going to be like for her when she grew up. She was only fourteen and according to her everyone had a problem.

Marsha had broad shoulders for a girl, and she had thick brown hair that she liked to shake when she sat down. She smoked a lot. Since she worked part-time in the Five and Dime Store, she always had cash with her.

She wasn't fat but she wasn't thin like Sarah either and occasionally I'd catch her looking at Sarah in an odd way. Nothing bad but like she found Sarah a mystery that she was trying to figure out.

One night me and Sarah were sitting side by side on a large dead tree and I asked her why she was Marsha's friend.

"Because of her cousin," she answered.

That was the first time I heard about Billy Dean. Marsha had an older cousin who lived in Saugerties who was *dreamy*.

Michael went to school and worked in a factory. He came by occasionally to see Marsha for some reason and that's how Sarah met him.

"I was like nine or something and just seeing him walk made me think of boys in a serious way."

I pretended to understand what she was saying and let her talk.

"He hangs with these guys. You know, tough guys from the south side and they are close to joining Hell's Angels," Sarah said.

I had heard of the motorcycle gang only from stories friends would tell back in the city. There weren't many motorcycle gangs in the city, but my best friend Frankie told me that there were gangs upstate.

"They don't care about anybody. Not the cops, nobody," Sarah said.

"What do they do for jobs?" I naively asked.

Sarah humored me though I thought I saw her cringe when I asked the question. "They don't *need* jobs," she answered. "They just ride their bikes, you know. They never stay in one place too long."

I didn't want to hear anything more about Billy Dean. I was getting jealous, and I didn't like the feeling. All I wanted to do was spend quiet time with Sarah and watch her just sitting on that dead tree.

I liked looking at Sarah more than any other girl I had ever met. In looking at her so much I noticed some things about her. Her thumb on her right hand was unusual. It was tiny and fat and was so cute I couldn't take my eyes off it.

She also had a habit of closing her hands when she talked and placing them on her lap. I wasn't sure if other girls did this, but I noticed her doing it and it mystified me. I liked looking at what she wore taking delight in the colors she picked knowing that she seemed to delight in the colors she picked.

She was very fond of this dark blue and gold paisley shirt she wore and let it hang over her blue jeans. It made her soft brown eyes look even softer and it made her look older.

I liked how it looked when she wore her white jeans, and I knew it would make me sound weird if I told her how much I liked it. But I did.

"I'll get you one when we go into Saugerties," she said.

I didn't know we had made plans to go into the town but I was thrilled to hear that she had thought about going with me. Just the notion that Sarah thought of me when I wasn't with her was something that I genuinely enjoyed.

I know it was odd, but I pictured us being married. I had no idea what it meant in real life, but I liked the thought of seeing her every day. I also liked how the wind blew her hair around her face and how it wrapped around her cheeks. When this happened, I could see her eyes glowing as if they were seeing only me.

One night she wanted to run with me through the field on the other side of the road. There was a half-moon hanging through the clouds and she wanted to race underneath it.

So, we ran into the summer breeze cutting through the shadows. Just the two of us alone with no one around for at least a half mile. Without man-made lights or cars ruining the night, it all seemed more real than anything I had ever done before.

We ran up a hill that was smooth with grass and eventually threw ourselves down lying back to look up at the night sky. We lay back for a long time and the only thing I could think of was how only a week earlier I hadn't even known Sarah and now she was the reason I got up in the morning. All I wanted to do was see her at night and spend that magic time with her.

"You light up the dark," I muttered embarrassed.

Sarah didn't say a thing, but she did reach for my hand and touched my fingers caressing them gently.

I never kissed anyone before and I wasn't about to. Physically the entire action was beyond my comprehension.

I heard her say something and it made me realize how much I liked her voice. I had noticed that when we were at the community center and she was speaking with the cousins or with Marsha she allowed her voice to be rough with an edge to it but with me it was melodious and even more than that she sounded wise beyond both our years.

Though we were under the stars without anyone else around we started whispering. I told her how the night was when I felt alive, and she told me that it was her favorite time also.

Somewhere in there she asked if I had heard anything from my mother. I told her I hadn't, and she looked sad.

"I'll hear from her," I said comforting her more than myself.

"I hope you do. You like your mother, and you can't lose her. It's hard to replace people you like."

I knew she was speaking about her father, so I again tried to reassure her. "I won't lose my mom."

After a short silence we discussed in length if we liked before midnight or after. I told her that I liked ten p.m. because the world got quiet even in the city.

She said she liked two a.m. because the world was asleep and none of her thoughts could be interrupted by anyone or anything else.

It was then that we made a pact that when we drove cross-country in my red Mustang we would travel only at night between the hours of ten p.m. and right before dawn and then sleep all day.

She told me that we would rent hotel rooms and eat in diners since she loved diners and that she would tell Billy Dean to meet us, and he could follow us on his motorcycle.

Just mentioning Billy Dean made me tense up. Sarah noticed that I was sulking. A wave of depression came over me and though I fought to ignore it, I couldn't.

I got up and walked down the hill towards waves of tall grass that were blowing in the wind.

"What's wrong, Chris?"

I couldn't tell her.

She then put her hand on my face. "I'm going to marry Billy Dean. I hope we can still be friends."

I turned my back on Sarah and walked away. She followed me for a while but then when I reached the cornfield I turned around and I saw that she was gone.

I went home to find my aunt asleep at the table on the porch and my uncle asleep this time in his favorite chair in the living room facing the black and white television set.

I decided not to go to my bed but sit outside facing a sleeping Stalin hoping my mother would come home so I could leave Old Bridge and never see Sarah ever again.

5

I told myself that I would stay away from Sarah but the very next day I went into the village with my aunt and ran into her with her mother. She gave me such a big smile when she saw me, I melted.

The Village of Old Bridge didn't even have a traffic light. It had a gas station, a grocery store and liquor store and that was it.

My aunt and her mother talked for a couple of minutes in front of the tiny grocery store when Sarah whispered to me, "Be at the center by sunset. We are getting scary tonight. We're going to Mister Burger's house."

I reached the community center at sunset and found Sarah and Marsha waiting for me with new plans for the night. We were all invited to the go-cart racetrack.

We all got to pile into one of the cousin's father's pickup truck and I got to sit next to Sarah though Marsha took up all her time by talking.

The humid air felt good on our faces when we were moving down the dark roads. When we arrived at the go-cart racetrack, I was surprised how small it was. There were parking lots back in Queens bigger than the go-cart racetrack.

The go-carts were driven under the mangy old lamp lights on a dirt field and with the way the dust settled over everything it all looked surreal to me. It was hard for me to imagine that driving the rusty, two-seater go-carts was an exciting event for people but in Old Bridge it was.

There were two dozen people in the stands, and they stood in the shadows like zombies drinking beer and shouting at the drivers. Most of the adults were fat and tired looking.

I didn't have any money so me, Marsha and Sarah watched the cousins drive around in circles when all I wanted to do was stand close against the fence with Sarah at my side.

Marsha nudged me over to get closer to Sarah and then spoke, barely being heard over the din from the go-carts wailing engines.

"Old man Burger killed his wife and his problem is that he still loves her."

"He killed his wife and he didn't go to jail?"

Sarah interrupted. "Nobody is sure he killed his wife but everybody thinks he buried her in his basement."

"And why would you want to go to his house?" I asked.

"Because it's really funny when he gets mad at us," Marsha said.

Well, after the cousins dropped us off at the community center Marsha continued to press me and Sarah to walk to Old Man Burger's house. We gave in and went.

The Burger house was in the opposite direction of mine so the woods we walked through were all new to me. There were more trees in these woods even though his house wasn't too far off the main road.

We reached a small hill and hid in the grass. We looked down on the Old Man Burger's front porch.

"There he is," Marsha said pointing to an old man sitting on a rocking chair with a large rifle on his lap.

"I always say he buried his wife in the swamp behind his house," Marsha told us.

"She could be in the basement but I doubt he killed her," Sarah said next.

"Did either one of you ever see her before he killed her?"

They both looked at me perplexed. "No," they answered in unison. I figured they hadn't.

"He's got a thing for Sarah," Marsha chimed in.

"You keep saying that" Sarah responded.

"We'll he does," Marsha said. "His problem is he can't hide it when he sees you in the village. Just the other week he smiled at you when you and your mother were comin' out of Smithy's with your groceries."

I gave Sarah a look of sympathy. She shook her head and gave Marsha a smirk.

"Everybody has a thing for Sarah," Marsha then said with a bite in her voice. She then glanced at me.

I wanted to tell her that *yes* I have a thing for Sarah but it was none of Marsha's business. And I also wanted to say that it seemed to me that Marsha had a *thing* for Sarah as well.

Marsha stood up. "Let's go down there and bug him."

"No way," Sarah said.

"You scared too?" Marsha said.

I scowled at Marsha insulted that she would think I'd allow myself to be called scared in front of Sarah.

"I'll do it."

"Let's do it then," Marsha said then got up and walked slowly down the hill.

Sarah didn't budge but I got up and followed Marsha down the hill towards the lawn.

"He's got a dog so be quiet," Marsha told me.

I looked back when I heard Sarah right behind me. "I hate riling that old man," she whispered. "He never hurt anybody."

A few seconds later, when we reached the lawn still undetected, Marsha faced the house and shouted, "Where did you bury your wife, Mister Burger?"

I looked at Marsha barely making her profile out in the dark.

I turned to the porch. Mister Burger was asleep in his chair. I heard him mutter something at first then his voice grew louder.

"Who's that?" His voice was harsh and gravelly. He slowly stood up.

I could see him in the porch light. He looked much like my Uncle Marty. He was burley with broad shoulders a white beard and messy gray hair falling from under his diesel truck drivers cap.

I could see his suspenders, bare feet and when he stood, he gripped his shotgun with both hands.

"We bet you buried your wife in the basement!" Marsha shouted.

"I loved that woman," he told the darkness.

"Love don't mean anything but hardship," Marsha said. "You killed her just the same."

"You lousy kids! I'll have my dog eat you all dead!"

With that Marsha turned sharply knocking Sarah down to one knee. It all happened so fast that I hardly moved an inch when I saw Mister Burger open his door and a large German Shepard emerged from inside the house.

Marsha was already up the hill when I grabbed Sarah by the arm and tugged her along.

"I'm okay," she said.

I knew she wasn't.

I had to resist the surge of fear racing through me as I ran up the hill all the while making sure Sarah was right at my side keeping pace with me. I had to slow myself down as I struggled to control my pumping heart and my legs from just flying through the night air.

I thought I heard the dog racing up the hill and gaining on us. Sarah moaned in fear and I stopped running thinking that the only way I could protect her was to stand in the way of her and the menacing dog. I was sure it was going to rip us both apart.

But just then I heard Mister Burger shout to the dog to come back down the hill. I didn't turn back so when I reached the top of the hill I waited for Sarah.

"You okay?"

"She hurt my leg."

I looked around and Marsha was nowhere to be found. All that lay in front of us was dark wooded shadows.

We both kept moving until we reached the road and raced across it. We then made our way into the field that led to her house.

Before we got there Sarah had to stop to catch her breath. She sat down on the ground and grimaced.

"She's crazy," she whispered.

"Can I help?"

She didn't say anything but took off her sneakers. She was barefoot and I could see the flesh in the slight light from the half-moon. I had to say that my heart stopped.

"It's my ankle."

I saw that it was her left leg. The one that was shorter.

I sat down next to her and rubbed her ankle. I wasn't sure why, but I thought it would help and it seemed to work.

"Thanks."

I rubbed her ankle some more. It didn't seem swollen. "I think it's only sprained," I told her. "I had that happen to me once playing ball. My mother rubbed it and it felt better after a while."

Sarah got up and adjusted her sneakers, keeping them open so she could walk without pressure. She took a few steps then leaned on me. "Let's go," she said.

As we walked, I felt her hand gripping my arm. "You waited for me."

"I wasn't going to leave you there."

"I know."

When we reached her house, she leaned up and kissed me on the cheek then I watched her make her way to her front door and into her house.

Walking home through the cornfield, passed the scarecrow under the canopy of the night sky I hardly felt the ground under my feet.

6

The next few nights I didn't see Sarah. I stopped by her house but when her mother answered she told me that Sarah was staying off her ankle. It did swell up and she couldn't walk on it. So, I left her house and while walking back to mine I stopped in the cornfield and looked up at her bedroom window hoping to catch a glimpse of her, but I didn't.

I went back to my house, and when I did I found my aunt on the phone with my father. I hung around the porch waiting to see if he wanted to talk to me. Eventually my aunt called me to the phone, and I took it from her.

"Your aunt says you're doing okay," I heard my father's concerned voice say.

"Where's Mom?" The question just shot out of me and took me by surprise.

"Your mother is fine. She's in Pennsylvania with her sister like we figured."

"When is she coming home?" I asked noticing my aunt sitting back on the porch sipping her highball.

My father hesitated and then I heard him force a cheerful tone in his voice. "In a little while. She's still angry with me. But I think she'll forgive me eventually."

He then asked me about how things were going and if I was okay and I told him that I was. I wanted to tell him about Sarah but I figured my aunt was listening, so I didn't.

He then promised me he was going to come up and visit around Fourth of July and we said our goodbyes and I hung up.

That night I felt the weight of being alone physically affect me. I didn't know what to do with myself. I tried thinking of reading my music book and thinking about buying a guitar but all I could think about was Sarah. I was becoming fonder of her in ways I hadn't felt before.

I even thought of calling her, but I didn't have her phone number. I also figured I'd have to tell her mother, who would answer the phone, why I was calling her in the first place.

I couldn't tell her that I missed Sarah so even if I had her phone number I couldn't call.

So, I sat out on the porch trying to talk with my aunt, but she slurred her words and eventually she fell asleep sitting up leaning her head down on her chest.

Watching her made me think of what it meant to be an adult and it worried me. None of the adults in my life were happy or certainly didn't seem it. My aunt and uncle tolerated one another more than anything else and my father and mother only seemed to be at odds with one another.

It made me wonder why anyone got married in the first place but then I thought of Sarah and knew that for us it would be different. First off, we wouldn't live in one place. With my red Mustang we'd drive all around and travel to wherever we wanted to go. Secondly, we got along so well we'd never have to drink or argue.

However, all my thoughts crumbled when I thought about what she had said about Billy Dean and how she was going to marry him. The only thing that saved me from complete depression was that I was hoping that since he was older, he had his own girlfriend and would leave Sarah to me.

I spent my time watching TV with my aunt. She loved watching *I Love Lucy* and *The Beverly Hillbillies,* but her favorite was *My Mother the Car.*

"These shows are so smart. I wonder who thinks them up? I bet you can write something for TV someday. You are young but I bet you could."

I pondered the thought, but it was difficult to figure me writing. I wasn't sure what that meant. I only knew I was getting restless and since it was Friday night I eventually made my way to Sarah's house asking for her. Her mother told me that she was able to walk normally again and had headed down to the community center.

Once again I heard the transistor radio blasting music and this time it was "Cara Mia" by Jay and The Americans.

When I finally reached the center I found Sarah standing on the rotting wood deck with her back to me in a heated conversation with Marsha. They were standing under the collapsed roof which was lit only by the strangled light from the road lamps. They were shouting at one another with the three cousins circling them all with stupid grins on their faces edging the girls on to fight.

I was about to step over to them when Marsha pushed Sarah back up against the rotting rail and though Sarah nearly fell I saw her regain her balance and with all of her might she pushed back at Marsha.

Marsha, the much bigger girl, then swung her arm all the way around hitting Sarah across her shoulder and this time knocking her down. Like a big cat, Marsha jumped on top of Sarah and pinned her to the deck and placing her knees on her shoulders she sat over her smacking her in the face.

I couldn't just stand there and watch so I quickly rushed behind Marsha and grabbed her by her shoulders pulling her off Sarah.

I felt one of the cousins put me in a headlock from behind me while another one stepped up to me from the side and punched me in the stomach.

When I was a young kid and got into fights, I remember never feeling much pain. I do remember feeling rockets of adrenaline shooting through my muscles and that was exactly what happened to me finding myself outnumbered by the cousins and seeing Sarah being smacked around by Marsha.

Finding reserves of strength, I didn't even know I had kicked one cousin right in the groin while I elbowed the one who had me in a headlock right in his solar plexus.

I was suddenly free, so I rushed to Marsha and pulling her by the hair I yanked her off Sarah, hearing her moan. I then picked Sarah up and both of us rushed down the rickety community center stairs racing off into the dark.

Once again we found ourselves running through the woods and quickly found ourselves laughing loudly. I wasn't sure why we were laughing but I figured it had something to do with the danger and the excitement of what had just happened.

I followed Sarah and we didn't stop running until we were deep into the woods far from the community center and the cornfield.

Eventually we stopped and huddled under an enormous tree. It was a humid night, and I was sweating right through my dark blue T-shirt.

Sarah was taking deep gulps of air when she pointed. "The creek is right over there."

We walked through a small path making our way in the dim light thrown down by the fading moon until we reached the creek.

Sarah pulled off her own sweating T-shirt and though it was dark I could see her skin shine in the moon's glow and then she pulled off her sneakers and jeans wearing now only her white panties.

Without saying a word to me she walked into the creek sinking first down to her knees and eventually to her waist.

"It's nice and cool," she said. "Come on!"

I took off my sneakers, my T-shirt and my jeans and followed her in.

The thought of walking into a dark murky creek didn't appeal to the city boy in me at all but since Sarah was beckoning me, I knew I had to follow her.

When I reached her, she was in water up to her chest leaning against a tree trunk. I huddled next to her afraid to even think what living creatures were in the liquid I was immersed in.

We waved our arms back and forth under the water allowing it to cool us with its gentle sweetness. In the dark, but with help from the moon's light, I could make out Sarah's eyes and her lips.

"I hope you don't mind me being naked on top," she said softly. "I don't think much of clothes, and I feel comfortable with you."

"It's okay." She had tiny breasts and even tinier pointed nipples from what I could see. I had never been that close to a half-clothed female before and it was beyond exciting. If she had asked me to sit in a lion's den with her at that moment I would have gladly obliged.

"What happened back there?"

"Marsha has a girl crush on me."

"What's that?"

"It's when a girl has a crush on another girl."

"Can that happen?"

"It can more than you know."

"I don't understand."

"She kissed me last summer. It was out of the blue. We were walking down the road one night just talking and then she stopped and kissed me on the lips. Then, like nothing happened, we kept walking. She never said another word that night and we never talked about it again but plain as day she has a crush on me."

I was learning a lot about people by hanging with Sarah since that was something I had never heard of let alone thought of before.

"You are prettier than her," I said.

She smiled. "Thanks for saving my butt again." She then reached her mouth up to mine and tenderly kissed me.

I felt her hand on my shoulder and I pulled her closer. She smelled sweet and for the first time I felt like I knew her though I wasn't even sure what that meant.

With her standing that close to me and with us holding on to one another in the spooky nighttime woods was for me an enlightening moment. I realized that growing up was allowing someone else's vulnerability to affect you and mean something to you.

I also felt tremendously awkward. I held Sarah and in doing so, I felt like a man but I wasn't exactly sure what to do next, so I smoothed down her hair and she buried her face under my chin.

"I have a crush on you."

"I know you do."

"It's not a girl crush."

She got quiet. "It's so perfect here," she whispered and I knew then that she wanted protection just as I wanted protection from the things we couldn't understand. Not knowing was the threat and nothing else.

We kissed a little more but mostly held each other until we felt it was time to step out of the creek and back into our clothes.

We held hands walking back over the road and into the cornfield. "This doesn't mean we're going steady," she said.

I was taken aback. "What *does* it mean?"

She looked up into my eyes. "I'm not sure *what* it means."

When we got to the edge of light from her house, we faced one another and kissed. It was a more meaningful and heartfelt kiss than those kisses back in the creek.

I felt like a man kissing a woman and it was familiar, overwhelming, and strange all at the same time.

Sarah then smiled turned and raced back to her house and I turned and headed back to mine.

She then appeared behind me. "Have you heard from your mom?"

It took me an instant to recover from the surprise. "My father heard from her. She's with her sister."

Without saying another word Sarah turned and disappeared back into the darkness.

7

That following Saturday morning Sarah and I took the bus into Saugerties. I was surprised how small the town was. I wasn't used to seeing people living in a town that had one traffic light and where cars drove through the entire town in about a minute.

Sarah and I told her parents and my Aunt Angie that were going into the town to see the new James Bond movie *Thunderball* but we really wanted to hang out and explore. What I didn't know was that Sarah was hoping to run into Billy Dean, who she knew hung out in the town on Saturdays.

We talked about my plan of driving cross-country in my Mustang and while walking through Saugerties I imagined how Sarah and I would pass through different cities being strangers to everybody else. But having each other to rely on, talk to and share and express our feelings, would make it all wonderful.

Sarah took me to a small record shop. I exaggerated about my guitar playing talents fantasizing how I would write songs for her and play them in the bars we came across on our cross-country trip.

While in the record shop she pointed out the first hippie I ever saw. He was tall and skinny, about twenty years old I figured, with a thick black beard and he had mangy dark hair popping out of a small brown hat.

He was wearing a purple shirt, jeans and sandals. A woman was standing next to him looking through the records. She was about his age and she had a long yellow dress on and was barefoot and carrying sandals.

She lifted her arm and I saw that she didn't shave her armpit.

"Gross," Sarah said when she saw.

They were very easygoing, and they were listening to the albums playing on the speakers in the record store. "Mr. Tambourine Man" was the song I recognized, and I was impressed by how gentle the hippie couple were compared to some of the other people in the store.

Most of the others were *hitters*. Hitters were tough-looking boys and girls who were in their late teens and older and who had greasier hair and slick jeans and boots. I could see that they were eying the hippie couple with smirks on their faces.

"The war on poverty, man," the hippie guy said to the girl.

"So strange to have a war on a thing and not a people, you know?"

"They call it a war. I wonder who gets killed. How do you kill poverty, you know?"

"The *man* has gotten really strange," the woman said.

"Are you people commies?" one of the hitters asked.

The hippie guy turned to them. "We are for peace, man."

"I got drafted, man, to fight for scum like you," one of the hitters said.

"Peace brother," the hippie guy said.

"Yes, peace," the hippie woman said.

The hippies quickly left the record store.

"Where they from?" one of the female hitters asked.

"New York City probably," someone said.

"Where all the scum like them live. And all the Black people too."

Hearing that, Sarah and I left the record store.

"That's why I hate it here. They hate everything that's not like them. Like their so friggin' special."

"They smelled."

"Who smelled?"

"The hippie couple."

"Yeah, I know. I think it's marijuana," Sarah said.

"It smells bad," I said.

We walked around the town. Sarah seemed increasingly preoccupied. When we got hungry we went to the diner and sat in a booth together ordering burgers and sodas.

I felt like a couple, and I wanted to tell her that her white button-down shirt with her blue collar looked cute. I didn't realize she wore it for Billy.

The day flew by so quickly and sometime around six in the evening Sarah suggested we walk to the bowling alley that was called Forty-Two Lanes.

When we got there, I saw over a dozen kids hanging out in the parking lot and Sarah had no intention of going inside to bowl. She wanted to hang out and as soon as she saw the kids, all of them older than us, she acted like she was hypnotized.

I was taken in by them too. The guys were mostly loud but all of them were just cool with their slicked back hair and their tight T-shirts mostly black and their straight legged blue jeans and boots.

The girls were women to me though none of them were even twenty yet. They were either quiet and pretty or laughing and playing around and pretty.

They wore tight jeans and tight T-shirts and some had their hair combed up and others were more natural but all of them were wearing makeup and it made Sarah uncomfortable.

She and I hung out near enough to the parking lot while at the same time clearly not secure enough to even pretend, we belonged there.

We bought bottled cokes and sat on the bench between the parking lot and the front door to the bowling alley transfixed by all the activity around us. Even when the local police car drove by we both enjoyed the same sense of danger and threat that the other teens caused.

When older couples showed up to bowl they shot nervous glances at the dozens of kids hanging out on the side of the building doing nothing scarier than drinking soft drinks and smoking cigarettes. But that was exactly what made them juvenile delinquents. However, that all ended when a deep brown Pontiac pulled up and most of the kids, recognizing the car, reacted.

The girls got quiet and the guys grinned especially when the driver and his passenger got out of the car. I had never seen Billy Dean before but I knew it was him.

He got out of the passenger car moving as if a glacier was weighing him down and he felt the entire continent as a burden of perplexity.

He was slim and lanky with a mass of dark blond hair combed up on the sides coming to a peak over his forehead. From where I stood, I could see the cigarette pack in his white T-shirt sleeve and how he hitched up his dark blue jeans around his waist. The look gave the impression that he was someone who thought a lot about everything. He didn't walk, he *moved*.

The driver was Michael Burbalack and he was just as impressive. He had a mass of dark hair and dark blue eyes and wore a black T-shirt and light blue jeans. He stood more upright like a brick wall and hung his face down just enough to make it look like he was sensitive but at the same time tough.

When Billy Dean and Burbalack walked toward the crowd everyone took notice. Sarah stood up and was speechless. I have no idea what it means to say when someone has presence, but I have to say that they both had it.

Billy's hooded light blue eyes found me for some reason, and I froze. It was because he saw Sarah and quickly looked at who she was with.

Even with all the other girls closer to his age smiling at him, he walked over to her first. He grinned when he reached her and winked at me.

"Hey, Mike, look who's here," he said.

Billy Dean's voice was just above the pitch of a heart murmur.

I thought I heard Sarah purr. She reached up and put her arms around his neck and buried her face in his chest.

"Take it easy little one," he said to her. "Who's this?" he asked her, nodding to me.

"Chris," she answered without looking at me. "We took the bus here."

"What did you want to do, Billy?" I heard a voice ask. It was Burbalack. He had a deeper sound to his voice than Billy. When he spoke, he sounded assured of what he was either asking or stating.

I looked up at him and saw two large dark blue eyes looking back at me. He had a small nose, ears, and lips though his chin was angular and sharp. His forehead was pronounced, and his black hair cut to a widow's peak accentuating his stare.

I had noticed but Billy Dean had an unlit cigarette in his mouth. It dangled there as he lifted Sarah off the ground. He lifted his head and nodded as he allowed all the other teens to focus on him without him acknowledging anyone else other than Sarah and me.

"Get some beers."

Burbalack nodded. "Shoot some pool?"

Billy Dean pushed his jaw together and his lips out showing without words that the thought didn't interest him.

Burbalack took his pack of cigarettes out of his short sleeve, knocked the pack against his right-hand knuckles to dislodge one and then lit it. He then took a drag. "It's Saturday night, man," he simply said.

Billy Dean smiled at Sarah. "It's Saturday night, man," he said mimicking Burbalack.

Burbalack took a drag on his cigarette. "I ain't spendin' my Saturday night with some kids."

"Chill, man," Billy Dean said. "It's cool." Billy Dean looked at us. "Mike here wants to burn his draft card tonight."

"Yeah," Burbalack said.

I was in awe. I wasn't exactly sure what it was they wanted to burn but it sounded primitive.

"There's a war on poverty," Sarah said sharply. She looked at me. "I just heard about it."

"And there's a war in Vietnam and I'm not going to die in some jungle for no gooks," Burbalack said.

"What's a gook?" I asked.

Billy Dean smiled. "VC, baby. The Viet Cong."

"But I ain't no draft dodger, get that straight. I'm not running to Canada either," Burbalack said.

"They can get us," Billy Dean agreed.

"I don't want them to get you," Sarah said.

"Who can get you?" I asked.

"Uncle Sam, kid," Billy Dean answered. "He can draft our assess and send us to boot camp and then send us off to get killed in some godforsaken jungle."

I could see Sarah cringe. "I don't want to see you go anywhere and get killed."

Burbalack spoke up. "My cousin Louis died there two months ago now. The Viet Cong bombed a hotel in Saigon, and he was just hanging out. He was just there on R & R."

"Yeah, my cousin Norm is in the Marines. He was deployed into the jungle for search and destroy missions. He wrote to me last week. He said it was hell, but we are going to win."

"The hell with fighting on the other side of the world I say," Burbalack said. "I'm going to burn my draft card."

"Five years in jail," Billy Dean said to him.

"Five years I'm *alive* with all my body parts," Burbalack said.

Billy Dean threw his tongue around his bottom teeth and then spit. "Okay, then let's blow," he said drolly.

He and Burbalack then turned around and walked back to their Pontiac.

"Where are you going?" Sarah asked.

"Just going," Billy Dean answered.

"Tell me where," Sarah pleaded.

Billy Dean leaned in and whispered something to her.

"Take me with you," Sarah said.

Billy Dean leaned back and pondered the notion for a moment.

"She's jailbait," Burbalack stated.

Billy Dean eyed Sarah. "Yeah, little one, you *are* jailbait. Stay loose," he told her and then both got into the car with Burbalack behind the wheel. They backed out of the parking lot and drove off through the town disappearing in seconds.

All the air left Sarah and I could see her entire being deflated. She looked pale to me, and I was worried.

"You, okay?"

"Let's go home."

We walked to the bus depot and sat on the bench. "He knows all about how things are. He knows how you can't get tied down to anything. He knows that you have to be ready to go anywhere and do anything. He knows all that and he shares that just by being himself," she said.

From the moment Billy Dean appeared I felt alone and Sarah was only there because her body was, but her heart and soul had left with him.

We sat on the bus together but again I could have been alone since all she did was look out the window and sulk.

I knew that it would get me nowhere if I tried talking to her and her silence pushed me into being depressed, something I didn't like to feel.

When the bus left us off in town, her mother was waiting for us and she talked about absolutely nothing important but to hear herself talk. She did this all the way to the cornfield where she left me off since that was what I asked her to do.

I didn't even say goodbye to Sarah but just opened the back door and got out and rushed off. I heard her mother ask, "Did you two have a fight or something?"

I didn't hear Sarah's answer and when I got home, I felt my aunt and uncle's house closing in on me. I sat out on the porch fighting off mosquitos happy at least to see that my aunt had gone to bed already.

I decided that night to call my father the next day to tell him I wanted to go home.

8

I called my father the first thing the next morning but there was no answer. My aunt saw how anxious I was, so she gave me a chore of cleaning out the backyard of all the weeds.

I got all kinds of bug bites doing it but in a way I was happy to keep busy. The sky was overcast and it was humid, and by late afternoon it stormed.

My aunt and I sat on the porch watching the storm approach. Where we sat we were blinded by the sun, but on the other side of the cornfield where Sarah lived there was a deluge with sheets of rain just pouring from the sky.

"Wow, it's raining down there and the sun is out here," I said to my aunt, mystified as I watched.

"Just wait," she said to me.

In a matter of a few minutes, I could see the sheets of rain moving towards us shutting out the light darkening everything. The wind came first rushing through the porch screen throwing the flies in a tizzy. Then the rain reached the center of the cornfield heading towards our house.

When the rain reached the porch, it came down in buckets. I watched it drench everything in its path.

It riveted me all. My aunt saw my fascination and grinned. "That is mother nature," she said to me.

She glanced at the clock. She then got up and went into the kitchen to make herself a highball.

Alone I looked out towards Sarah's house. Though I couldn't see it exactly I did know where it was. It was nestled in the hills to the left of the cornfield from where I was sitting.

My thoughts went to Sarah and how I had spent the entire day thinking about her and how I was going to miss her since I had no plans to go to the community center.

I began thinking of my life and friends back in Queens and how I wished my good buddy Frankie was with me so I could share my experiences with him but what I really wanted to talk about was Sarah.

The rain rushed over our house and disappeared quickly and a short time later the sun came out and thanks to the hot and humid air all the rain that fell on the cornfield, the trees and grass just disappeared as well.

After dinner both my uncle and aunt followed their routine. He fell asleep in front of the TV, and she continued with her highballs but this time she fell asleep knitting.

I don't remember the exact time, but I couldn't stop myself so I took a walk through the cornfield and stopped by Sarah's house.

When I got there I stayed in the shadows trying to get a glimpse of Sarah so I could go over and see her. However, when I got there, I saw her mother's car drive up and when she got out she saw me facing the house at the edge of the light.

"Is that you, Chris?" she asked while slamming the door shut.

"Yes," I answered stepping closer.

"I was about to drive to your aunt's house. Have you seen my daughter?"

I was surprised by the question. "No."

"Oh," she mumbled. She didn't move. "I've been down the community center and none of the kids have seen her."

I walked closer and stopped near to her car. "I last saw her last night when you dropped me off."

"You haven't seen her all day then?"

"No." I saw that she looked worried.

"I haven't seen her since last night either. I was up early with my husband to drive to church this morning. I didn't think of checking her bedroom since she never goes with us. When I got home, I saw that she never went to sleep."

Of course, the first thing I thought of was Billy Dean and whatever it was that he had whispered to Sarah. Perhaps he told her where he was going and to meet him there?

Sarah's mother walked over to me and it was the first time I was face to face with her.

She was taller than me with a white puffy face and big round eyes that at that moment looked sad and murky. She was fat and I could see the bulge of flesh slightly rippling out of her pink T-shirt.

"She said you two were good friends. Did she say anything to you on where she was thinking of running away to?"

"She never said anything about running away," I lied still wondering if Sarah ran away with Billy Dean.

"Tell me the truth, Chris. I know you two talked. And I want to tell you that she really doesn't like living here with her stepfather," she said.

"I didn't know that." I lied again.

Sarah's mother now moved away from me and looked out into the dark field that seemed to spread out from her front door in all directions.

"This isn't really a good place for a girl like Sarah to grow up in. She's full of energy and always looking for an adventure and this is the middle of nowhere really."

I pretended to be sympathetic and though I was I had no idea what I could say to make her feel any better.

"Sarah wants to live with her father but he doesn't want her."

This got my interest since it was the exact opposite of what I was led to believe from Sarah herself.

"His new girlfriend has no interest in Sarah living with them," she told me. "I tried to keep that information from my daughter 'cause I know it would hurt her to know the truth."

With that she turned and walked back to the house. "Maybe she'll come home tonight." She then looked directly at me. "I know you're a good kid so if you see her tell her to please come home."

I watched how she then walked into the house and closed the door.

I didn't bother going to the community center knowing that whatever I heard would be nothing but gossip. Instead, I went back to my aunt and uncle's house and sat in front of the black and white television and watched the Yankees play.

When the game was over, I went up to my room but there wasn't much to do so I sat by the window breathing in as much of the breeze that I could catch. It was another warm and humid night and the air hung so heavily it was hard to get comfortable.

Eventually I took off my jeans and T-shirt and lay on the bed, but I kept the light on, and I was glad that I did because I heard a rock hit the windowsill and jumped up to see who threw it.

I went to the window and saw Sarah standing right at the edge of the light above and behind Stalin's doghouse. She was petting Stalin and waving to me at the same time.

I quickly got dressed again and rushed out of my room quietly down the stairs and out the back door.

*

Sarah and I walked down a road I hadn't walked down before. It was behind my aunt and uncle's to the right of Stalin's doghouse. It was made mostly of hard dirt and clay and led to what Sarah said was a cement quarry.

There were very few trees, so we walked over the hard dirt for a long while under the hazy night sky. It didn't seem so dark to me, so I figured I was getting used to the country at night. We eventually reached a rusty abandoned car sitting near a small dirt hill.

"That's the swamp," Sarah told me pointing to some smooth-looking watery concoction populated by reeds that bent in the gentle breeze.

We sat down on the hard dirt next to the abandoned car in silence; the same silence we shared on our walk.

"I saw your mother," I told her. I then explained the how and why of my pronouncement. Even in the dark I could see Sarah cringe.

"Where were you?" I asked.

She then explained how she snuck out of the house right after her mother and stepfather went to bed. She hitched hiked back to Saugerties looking for Billy Dean.

I was right about him whispering in her ear. That as when he told her where to meet him.

"I don't want him to die in Vietnam and I'd never see him again."

"He might not get drafted."

"He will."

"If he goes to fight it doesn't mean he'll die."

"But he can die and I can't even imagine that."

Sarah then told me what had happened next. Billy Dean and Burbalack drove to the lighthouse where a lot of the older kids hung out on a Saturday night. Sarah eventually made it there and, in the dark, found the Pontiac but she couldn't find Billy Dean until sometime right before dawn.

When she did find him he was drinking beer with his arm around some slut as Sarah called her. He also laughed when Sarah jumped on the girl and punched at her missing most of the time but eventually the older girl had enough and smacked Sarah hard across the face.

Billy Dean didn't like that so he got up, and without saying a word to either girl, he walked away. He walked along the dock away from the lighthouse with his beer in hand and a cigarette dangling in his mouth. Sarah told me that eventually she caught up to him near a small dock and they both sat down and talked until the sun came up.

When the sun did come up Burbalack found them together and he shouted at Billy Dean that they would both get in trouble if they got caught with an underaged girl.

This time they put her in the Pontiac and drove her to the bus depot and gave her enough money to take the bus back to Old Bridge.

"He loves me, I know he does," she told me.

"How do you know that?"

"I can tell. A girl can tell about those things."

"Why did you come to me tonight?"

She explained to me that she needed a place to sleep. She had a plan. She was going to sneak back into her house, get all her clothes, borrow money from her mother, though she was really going to steal it, and take a bus to Albany.

"Why Albany?"

"I told Billy Dean that I'd meet him up there. I told him I'd be on the steps of the capital building at midnight tomorrow night."

"You told him that?"

"I sure did."

"And what did he say?"

"He didn't have to say anything. I know he'll be there."

"You didn't answer me. Why did you come to me tonight?"

This time she looked at me. I could see her soft eyes in the little light there was. I could see the outline of her profile looking into a future I'd not be a part of.

"I was going to ask you two things. One, if you can find a place for me to sleep tonight in your aunt and uncle's house and second if I can borrow some money from you for my trip. Of course, I'll pay you back. Billy Dean has a job, so we are good for it."

I struggled not to be flustered. I didn't want to tell Sarah that Billy Dean was not to be trusted. I didn't want to remind her that she had promised to go cross-country with me in my red Mustang.

"You can stay in my room and sneak out after my uncle leaves for work," I blurted out.

She quickly leaned in and kissed me tenderly on my cheek and then sat back in my lap placing her head against my stomach.

"My aunt gets up with my uncle, but she goes right back to bed once he drives away," I told her. "I don't have much but you can have it."

We sat in silence for a long time when I realized that Sarah had fallen asleep. Sitting there in the dark made me feel like I was sitting on the dark side of the moon. If Sarah wasn't with me I'd be so scared I'd run off and never look back.

I didn't want to move because I didn't want to wake her, so I thought long and hard about telling her mother of her plans.

It wasn't that I didn't trust Billy Dean, but I had a bad feeling about her running away without telling her family. Also, knowing what her mother had told me about how her father didn't want her to live with him made me realize how little Sarah really knew about the world.

I guess for the first time in my short life I was beginning to learn that there were people who knew how to deal with terrible things that came their way and there were others who just didn't. I wasn't sure which one I was but I was beginning to realize that Sarah was one of those who had no idea how to navigate the pitfalls of adulthood.

I also thought about how some people are lucky in life and some aren't. I also thought how some people are just born cool and Billy Dean was a prime example. There was just something about him that made it seem that life was just one big ocean, and he knew how to swim gracefully through it and that gift just came naturally.

I thought of myself as someone who had to learn and maybe that made me smart, but Sarah was another story. She was so special in my mind but also so vulnerable. Thinking that about her made me hold her tightly for a long moment.

I unintentionally woke her up and in minutes she was awake enough to walk back to my aunt and uncle's house.

We tiptoed upstairs to my room and I told her to lay down on the bed, which she did and she quickly went back to sleep. I figured she hadn't gotten any sleep in the last day and night so it was good for her to rest.

I sat in the chair beside the bed and just looked at her until, I too, felt sleep crawl up from my feet to my chest and then into my eyes.

9

Stalin's bark woke me up and I opened my eyes to see Sarah asleep beside me. We both were fully dressed lying on top of the bed sheet since it was so warm.

I looked at the clock on my night table and saw that it was just before seven and figured that my uncle must have left for work already. I was hoping that my aunt might be back in her bed.

I got up and walked out of the room trying not to wake Sarah and checked to see if my aunt's bedroom door was closed. It was and though every time I walked on the hard wood floors, they creaked. I made it back to my room and sat on the bed next to Sarah without waking anyone.

I let Sarah sleep a few minutes more before waking her. When I whispered her name she opened her eyes and looked at me as if she had been in a deep dream and was now emerging from it.

I could see thoughts fly across her eyes, far away thoughts and not all of them particularly good ones when she then asked, "Do you think you'll hear from your mother today?"

I wasn't sure why she asked but I quickly told her that I hoped that I would and that she had to get up and that we had to leave.

We rushed out of the house as quietly as we could and when we reached the old mushroom barn which was on the other side of the small bridge I turned to look back at the house.

I wanted to make sure my aunt didn't see us. The house was all lit up from the rising sun with speckles of bright white light exploding off the windows so if my aunt was watching I couldn't tell. Satisfied that we were fine I took Sarah's hand and edged her into the shadows.

The mushroom barn was a real barn decades earlier but fell to disrepair and decay and now it was filled with wild mushrooms. Thousands upon thousands of mushrooms grew everywhere in the damp, dark barn. When you stepped inside you could see them, some a foot high, growing from the visible dirt, some from the rows of wooden rafters and some upside down from what was left of the roof.

I imagined it was because the overhanging tree limbs that covered the entire barn prevented any sunlight from ever reaching the interior. That darkness created a damp, dank shadowy world: a perfect breeding ground for mushrooms.

I hadn't been near the barn since my arrival. I found the place spooky.

"I saw bats fly out of here at night sometimes when I was down this way," Sarah told me as I handed her all the cash, I could give her. She took it and placed it in her side pocket of her tight jeans and looked back up at the barns rafters and shook her head ever so slightly. "So many places in the world are so dark and mysterious," she said. That was the last thing she said to me before she kissed me on the right cheek and ran out of the barn, out onto the road and up the hill.

I watched her race up the gravel road covered with gray rocks then through the smaller trees until I lost her in the deep marvelous green that flowed like a fountain from the trees and ground.

I had taken her into the barn to hide while I gave her the money. I also took her into the barn to have her for myself for a few last moments before she left me behind. Once she was gone, I felt helpless and lost. I went back to the house and sat down with Stalin until sleep overcame me.

My aunt found me asleep with Stalin licking my face and she made me breakfast and if I can recall that day exactly, I could honestly say that nothing exciting happened the rest of it. I helped my aunt with her chores, got a call from my father asking me how I was doing and then had dinner with my aunt and uncle.

While on the phone my father had told me that my mother had asked about me and wanted to talk to me. He told me that she was going to call that night and she did.

It was after dinner and the night air was humid and a fog appeared coming down from the mountains to the north and huddled in the valley. It was so thick I could hardly see the cornfield.

I was standing in the living room with the black phone in my hand with the extension coming from the wall looking out at the fog when I heard my mother on the other end.

"Hi, Mom," I said.

It sounded like she was crying but I wasn't sure. She quickly told me how much she had missed me and that she was hoping to work everything out with my father and come home.

I asked her what had to be worked out, but she really didn't explain other that it was an *adult problem.* She then asked me how my summer had been so far and I was about to tell her about Sarah when I realized that it wasn't something I could explain. So, I told her that my summer was okay and that I was looking forward to seeing Frankie and my other friends back home.

"Are you and Pop getting together again soon?" I asked.

She was quiet on the phone and then told me that she loved me, that she would see me soon, and then asked for my aunt and I pushed open the screen door and went outside.

I hated the fog. With Sarah gone off somewhere I felt a profound loneliness. Of course, looking back, I'm not sure what that profound loneliness was to a thirteen-year-old but at that time it certainly felt profound.

I watched some television show with my Uncle Marty and watched as he fell asleep as if the sound emanating from the small black and white screen was his clarion call to leave his consciousness and go off and dream.

I then went to my aunt who was on her third or fourth highball and I watched her play solitaire until she too disappeared from the conscious world dipping her head onto her chest. I listened to her breathing deeply while her chest heaved up and down to the rhythm of whatever internal and bodily music to which she was listening.

I eventually went to my room and thought about Frankie and the guys and hanging out in the park and how far away that world was at that exact moment in time and space. I fell asleep thinking of Sarah.

I can't honestly recall but quite sure I did.

When I woke up I found my aunt standing over me. "There's a police officer at the door. He wants to speak with you."

A few minutes later, groggy and confused, I found myself face to face with a very tall county sheriff's deputy. He had a crew cut, keen dark eyes and a large beige cowboy hat.

I stood on the porch, and he was on the other side of the screen and he asked me to step outside. My aunt lingered behind me.

"Chris, I'm Deputy Lawson. I'd like to ask you a few questions about Sarah Viola. She lives up the road in that house on the other side of the cornfield.

"Sure," I told him.

"Her mother said she thought you were with her last night."

"I saw her the night before I think. Not last night though," I lied.

"Well, her poor mother is worried."

"How come?" I asked.

"Sarah is missing. For two days now. Did she tell you anything about her running away or anything like that?"

"No," I lied again.

"Do you have any idea where she might be?" I got the feeling that he didn't believe me and if he didn't, I got the feeling it didn't much matter to him that a teenage girl had run away. Looking back now I figure for him it must have happened a lot. Teenage girls looking for adventure and running away from the mundane lives they witnessed their parents living. I knew that was exactly what Sarah feared because she just as much told me so.

"Well, if you hear from her let me know," he said.

I watched him walk back down the hill to his deep brown and gray patrol car which matched the colors of his uniform.

I continued to stand there watching him drive away down the gravel road and passed the mushroom barn and into the thick green foliage.

"Breakfast will be ready," my aunt told me.

Not long after that we were both at the table on the porch eating our ham, eggs and toast looking into the hazy morning sunshine and I was thinking of Sarah and her trip to Albany. I imagined her meeting Billy Dean and wondered what would happen next for her.

I wondered if they'd get in his car and drive to Canada or even down to Mexico. It was all exciting to think about if it were Sarah and me and not, she and Billy Dean.

"Why did you lie, Chris?" my aunt asked me.

I looked at her across the table.

"Why did you lie to the deputy sheriff?" she asked as she sat back in her chair. For the first time I noticed how pretty her large round blue eyes were. In the morning light they were a soft blue gray with tints of yellow here and there in the pupils.

I also noticed the streaks of gray and yellow in her hair and the large sacks of crumbled skin under those colorful eyes.

"What do you mean, aunt?" I sheepishly asked.

"I saw you leave the house early yesterday morning with Sarah Viola. Did she sleep over?"

I barely managed to nod.

"I saw you both walking to the mushroom barn. Then I saw her go up along the road up the hill by herself. I saw you linger in the barn and then come home."

My aunt was oddly reasonable and coherent that morning. I had been used to her downing her highballs and underestimated her succinct demeanor when she wasn't drinking.

"Why not tell the deputy sheriff the truth?"

I lowered my fork onto my plate. I wasn't sure what to answer.

"Are you protecting her from something?"

I was sad that my aunt had to witness me lying and sad that I got caught. "I didn't want to tell on her."

"Tell on her?" she asked leaning forward.

"She was running away."

"To where?"

"Albany. She was going up there to meet Billy Dean."

"Who is he?"

"The guy she likes," I said feeling a weight lifted from my shoulders.

"How would she get there?"

"I gave her some money for a bus."

My aunt didn't say anything for a few moments. She lingered at the table and then left the porch and went into the kitchen. When she came back, she took away the plates. "We'll tell papa tonight at dinner and see what he suggests we do."

That night my aunt did tell my uncle and he wasn't pleased. "Never lie to the police, boy. Unless it's something to do with the family. If it's family that you are protecting than it's not a lie. It's what we call a *white* lie. But this with the Viola girl has nothing to do with family."

I listened closely perplexed by the logic but certainly understanding that I was in trouble.

He sat quietly for a few moments eying his pork chop and then pushed his jaw together, released it then spoke. "Mama, you bring the boy down to the sheriff's office first thing tomorrow morning and you," he said, looking at me, "you tell them all you know about this girl and her running away," he stated. Satisfied that he had made the right decision he proceeded to devour his dinner.

The next morning, I sat in the Saugerties Sheriff Department's office facing the sheriff himself. He was a large man not much unlike my uncle Marty except he had gray hair that flowed over his head as if someone cracked an egg on it.

He wore silver rimmed glasses, and he had a white mustache. He first asked my aunt a lot of questions about me and why I was visiting her.

My aunt got dressed for the interview. She wore a flowery yellow print dress and combed her hair back with a ribbon in it.

Of course, like my uncle told me the night before, you only lie for your family so my aunt did just that. When she explained why I was visiting her she left out the part of my mother running away and told the sheriff that I was spending some time in the country just to get away from the city.

The sheriff seemed knowledgeable on the notion of *getting away from the city* so he quickly took her explanation as the truth.

He then turned and questioned me with a pleasant tone to his voice. I quickly told him all I knew and blushed when I explained how I gave Sarah what money I had saved for the summer.

"What did she need the money for?" he asked.

I told him that she was planning to take a trip to Albany but when he asked me who she was going to meet in Albany I lied again and didn't say anything about Billy Dean.

"They always run away for a boy," the sheriff sputtered out.

I don't know why I was protecting Billy Dean or if I was protecting him at all. I lied to protect Sarah. In my teenage mind I knew she was making a bad choice in choosing him and I wanted to protect her reputation. At least looking back that is what I was doing.

The sheriff thanked me for the information telling me that Sarah's mother would be relieved to know where Sarah had gone. He also told my aunt that they would alert the police in Albany to look out for Sarah. Her being underage would be a problem for any boy she was running away to meet. He then told my aunt that Sarah would eventually be found sooner rather than later. He didn't realize how wrong he was.

Later that night while keeping her company on the porch my aunt opened her purse and handed me twenty dollars. It was to replace the money I had given to Sarah. She told me that I was foolish but that my heart was in the right place.

She then looked directly at me and said, "I hope you told the whole truth to that sheriff."

She knew I hadn't.

10

The next week at my aunt and uncle's house was unexciting and painfully dull. I struggled to keep myself entertained.

One afternoon I asked my aunt if I could use the phone to call my friend Frankie. Of course, she let me but when I did call his mother answered only to tell me that he had gone to a Met's game with his father. I was completely jealous.

All was dreadfully quiet for a teenage boy living in a rural landscape where nothing exciting was happening. However, one afternoon, I saw a county sheriff's police car drive down the road to Sarah's house.

I rushed across the cornfield in hopes that I'd see Sarah being brought home. I knew she'd be upset about being brought home, but I was thrilled that she was home at last.

When I reached the house, I waited out in the field and saw the county sheriff's car parked in front. Then I heard a bone chilling scream. I waited until the deputy sheriff stepped out of the house. It was the same deputy sheriff who questioned me.

I stood back. He waved me over. I hesitated but eventually I did walk over to him.

"Your name is Chris, right?" he asked. His voice resonated through the sunshine.

"Yes, it is," I answered.

"The boy I questioned already?"

"Yes."

He looked passed me towards my aunt and uncle's house as if he were making a mental note to himself and then he looked back at me.

"That was her mother you just heard," he said.

I had no idea what to expect. "Sarah's home?"

"No, son. She isn't home. They found her shirt in a trash can near the lighthouse."

"How do you know it was her shirt?"

Just then her mother pushed open the screen door and walked towards us. She was wearing a white apron and a ballooning blue jeans skirt.

She was holding a shirt in her hands. The closer she got to me the more she held it up so I could see it.

"Who did this to her?"

I lowered my head but I wanted to see the shirt, so I continued to keep my eyes on the horizon.

"Was it you?" she growled.

"I didn't do anything to Sarah," I quickly explained.

I felt the deputy sheriff's eyes on me. I looked up at him and I could still see the look of suspicion.

"Why did you lie to me the first time I asked you about her?"

"I don't know."

It was then I saw the dark blue and gold paisley shirt. It *was* Sarah's.

Her mother held it up. It was ripped down the back. "Answer me," she demanded.

I wanted to turn around and run but all I could do was stand there. I know now I didn't run because I wanted to know where Sarah was as much as her mother did.

"We will be talking some more about this, son," the deputy sheriff said as he walked to his car and then drove away.

I'll never forget the look on Sarah's mother's face that day. Her big eyes were mirrors of her grief, her anger and her questions.

I went back to the house and sat down at the table. My aunt saw me from the kitchen and joined me. She asked me what had happened and in slow well-chosen words I told her about Sarah's mother's scream, Sarah's shirt being torn in the back and how the deputy questioned me again.

"I guess you have some explaining to do. What haven't you told *me*?"

"I didn't tell you about how Sarah told me she was going to go to Albany to meet Billy Dean."

*

The next day I told the sheriff what I had told my aunt. I told him while sitting in his office next to my aunt. She was bathed in the glare from the early morning sunshine.

"Why did she want to see him?"

"She was afraid he would be drafted to Vietnam and die fighting in the Army. Or Marines. He didn't say."

"Tall, lanky boy with blond hair?" the sheriff asked.

"Yes, sir."

"Would you recognize him if you saw him?"

"Yes, sir."

"Come with me."

I looked to my aunt who nodded for me to follow the sheriff.

I did what I was told. I was led to a door.

"I'm going to open the door and you tell me that the boy sitting in the chair in that room is him or not. Got it?"

"Yes, sir."

The sheriff opened the door.

Billy Dean was sitting in a chair at a table. When the door opened, he turned to me. "I didn't do anything to the girl. Why did you think I did anything?" he blurted out to anyone who would listen.

The sheriff shut the door and turned to me.

"Is that the boy you said she said she'd meet?"

"That is Billy Dean, yes."

He looked at my aunt. "Okay, he can go home now."

I felt the intensity of the precinct and the energy that was invisibly inching through every pore of the place. I was disappointed when my aunt hurried me outside.

That night at the dinner table my uncle questioned me as intensely as the sheriff had. He asked me everything from how I knew Sarah to how much I knew about Billy Dean. From the way his eyes narrowed when he looked at me, I had an idea that he wasn't happy with my involvement in the entire episode.

I told them both everything that had happened down to the minute detail of Sarah and me and our kissing in the woods. That night I hardly slept and when I woke up all I could think about was the look on Billy Dean's face.

I spent the day doing chores for my aunt and sometime after lunch I saw a police car drive down the road to Sarah's house.

I raced across the cornfield stopping at the house and then waited. I hadn't seen anyone for a long time. I felt the sun on my face, and I could hear bugs crackling and buzzing around in the tall grass.

I didn't want to be seen but I desperately wanted to know if they had found Sarah's body. I felt like I was in some kind of twilight zone helpless and confused.

The deputy sheriff then stepped out of the house. He saw me but looked toward his car instead. I stepped out of the tall grass so I was sure he could see me.

This time he did. "The mystery is over."

I wanted to know more but before I could say anything Sarah stepped out of the house.

Our eyes locked. I thought I was seeing a mirage in the bright sunlight. But it was her. She was gaunt and listless. Her mother rushed up behind her and pulled her back into the house before either one of us could speak.

I heard the sheriff deputy's patrol car drive down the road behind me and I turned realizing that no one was interested in telling me what happened. I stood in the cornfield looking up for a long time at her bedroom window. I didn't care who saw me. I felt relief, happiness and fulfilment knowing that she had been found unharmed.

Just as I turned to leave, I thought I saw a flicker of movement at her window. The sunlight bathed the side of her house, so I had to move to my left to get a better look.

I saw her. She was standing in the window. She waved. I smiled. She smiled back.

I went back to my aunt and uncle's house and found out that my mother was coming to visit me later that week.

11

I had just finished lunch with my aunt when we saw a car off in the distance on the road heading towards the house.

"That must be her," my aunt said.

It was a sunny afternoon when I found myself face to face with my mother. I was standing in front of the porch with the bright sunshine in my face.

She was dressed in blue with a tiny blue and white hat. It was warm yet she tried to look extra pretty for me.

I could see the outline of her face in the glow of the yellow light behind her.

My aunt hugged her, and they talked a little and the next thing I knew my mother and I were walking along the road.

She had driven up alone in a big maroon colored Pontiac with big tail back fins. I had never seen the car before.

"Whose car?"

"My friend's. He drove me here from Pennsylvania."

"Where is he?"

"In a motel off the thruway."

We walked along the dirt road and the small bridge that crossed over the small creek. The creek was dry.

"I miss you," she told me.

"Then why aren't you home?"

"Your father and I aren't getting along well."

"Why not?"

"Lots of reasons."

"Who cares that you're not getting along well?"

My mother's voice was feminine and sturdy. It was soft in tone but direct. When she spoke, I heard a person, not just my mother. There was nothing whiny or indecisive about her and that was reflected in her speech.

Unlike my father who spoke in staccato rhythms. He also didn't always pronounce all his words and he mumbled a lot unlike my mother who said every word effectively and clearly.

That afternoon I thought of something I hadn't thought of before. I wondered why they were together in the first place. Why were they even married?

I compared them to me and Sarah, and I saw a significant difference. Sarah and I had a lot more in common and more than that, I learned from her. I doubted my father let himself learn anything from my mother.

"I want to go home," I said.

"Not yet."

"Why not?"

"Your father can't take care of you alone."

"You can take care of me."

My mother stopped walking. She looked at me directly. She had oval shaped hazel-colored eyes, rounder than my father's.

She had fair skin and brown hair that fell across her shoulders. I was always surprised how long it was and only saw its entire length when she didn't tie it back. Like that afternoon it was silky and wavy as it cascaded down her neck. Her pretty face was round, heart-shaped and her nose was delicate.

"I'm not going back to your father."

I could hear the firmness in her voice that overrode any concern on how I would react to her announcement.

I noticed a tall, full tree in the near distance over her shoulder. It was a lush green with thousands of healthy leaves and its strength startled me.

"Then don't go back to him and take me with you."

"I want that. I do."

"So, what's wrong?"

"It will be a long time. You see, we must get lawyers and get divorced first. That will take time. Then your father might not let me have you and we will have to share you."

"Share me?"

"You will live with me and with him. I'm not sure if that is good for you. I don't know if you will like where I live now in Pennsylvania. I live with Aunt Jane. You know your Aunt Jane. My sister has three kids of her own right now. Plus, there's this friend I told you about who drove me here. A nice man. Jim. He's a good man. A widow. His wife died just two years ago. I know you would like him."

"Why do I have to like him?"

"I'm going to marry him."

"You are already married to Dad."

"Yes, that is why I have to get a divorce."

I was confused. I walked on alone. She let me walk alone for a little bit then followed.

"I know this must be tough for you. But you are my little man and I know you will be able to handle it. For me you will be able to manage it. I know you will."

My mother took my hand and walked me back to the car. "I have to drive back now," she told me. "I will call you in a few days. We're more than halfway through the summer now. You must get ready for school. I will come see you back in Queens before you go."

"I will see you again?"

"Of course," she said. There must have been something in the tone of my voice because she hugged me tightly in a way she hadn't before.

I watched her say goodbye to my aunt who appeared out of nowhere, then got into the car and drove away.

I watched the Pontiac make a U-turn and then head down the road disappearing into the tall, lush trees at the hill next to the mushroom barn.

I stood perfectly still. I didn't cry. I did nothing as I waited for her car to emerge out of the trees and appear on the road heading into the sunlight.

I felt a hand on my shoulder. "You are a tough soldier, boy," my aunt said.

I could see the sun reflect off the Pontiac as it drifted slowly away. Specs of silver light jumped up off the car and then it was gone.

*

Just as my mother left Sarah reappeared. I was walking through the cornfield that same night feeling alone. I was thinking to myself that it would have been better if I had never left the city and that my mother and father got along. It was a strange feeling realizing that your mother was not living in your own house anymore.

Meeting Sarah had been the highlight of my summer and even the year and now she was also gone. Until that night.

"Chris!"

I stopped. All around me were stalks of corn.

"Chris, over here," I heard.

I knew it was Sarah calling me.

She jumped out from behind a stalk and hugged me.

"Hi!"

Our faces were bathed in moonlight. Her hair had grown longer and now fell further down her shoulders. She was wearing a dark blue shirt and jeans.

"I snuck out."

"You're crazy,"

"I couldn't take being cooped up anymore. I saw you from my window. I had to see you."

She took my hand and we walked through the rows of tall corn and headed away from my aunt's house and toward the stone quarry.

We walked out of the cornfield where she took me to this perfectly large white slab of stone, and we sat down.

"My stepdad's out driving somewhere, and my mother is at her friend's house on the other side of the big hill. I got some time, so I figured I'd get out. I took the phone off the hook too, so she thinks I'm on the phone."

"You look so good," I told her.

"I missed two people. Billy Dean and you."

I sulked then perked up.

"I saw your mom today. She is pretty. I saw you and her walking and talking. Is she taking you back home?"

"No. She met another guy."

"Wow. I wanted to sneak out and see you since I was sure she was going to take you back to the city."

"She wants a divorce."

"Oh, man."

"I know."

"I learned from my father that you can only get a divorce in New York State by proving adultery."

"What's that?"

"She has to be cheating on your father with another man."

"That must be Jim. Her new friend."

We walked some more when I saw something large in the distance. I couldn't make out the shape in the dark and since the bright moonlight was falling across it at an angle its shape was hard to decipher.

"That's the bus."

I hadn't been down this far toward the rock quarry and I didn't know that there was a road that led to the back of my aunt and uncle's house.

We walked up to the bus. It was a VW Deluxe Micro Samba Tinnibus. It was facing away from my aunt and uncle's house towards the rock quarry. It looked so surreal sitting there on the dirt road among some small weed trees and foot high concrete mounds.

"How did this get here?"

"Nobody knows for sure. It's only been here since last summer. It was all covered in snow the last time I saw it."

I moved around it, looking up at the large windshield.

"It's like a spaceship from Mars that landed here."

"Marsha said it was from Europe. Or her father told her. We think some tourists drove down from Canada and left it here."

"Why would they do that?"

"Marsha said that they robbed a bank and used it as the getaway car."

"That's silly."

"It works. Anyway, it did last summer. You want to take it for a ride?" she asked. "I drove it down the road last summer with Marsha. I drove it down and then she turned it around and drove it back here. That's why it's facing this way. I bet the keys are still inside."

She jumped through the door and checked. "Yep, they are."

"Let's take it cross-country," I said. I wasn't sure where that came from but when I was around Sarah I thought all kinds of crazy things.

"I like that idea."

"We will need gas."

Sarah jumped in. "It's crazy but there's a full tank in there."

I could see her smile from ear to ear. With her face lit by the moonlight she looked like an angel sitting behind the wheel.

She turned the key and the engine started. In moments it was humming softly no louder than a lawn mower.

"Tomorrow night," she said.

"Tomorrow night."

She then shut down the engine and jumped back out. She rushed over to me and kissed me on the cheek just like my mother had and we walked back to the cornfield.

"Just to Saugerties."

"What?"

"Tomorrow night. We'll take it just to there first. Before we go cross-country."

"Can you get out?"

"I'll sneak out. *I Love Lucy* is on, and my mother never misses it. Let's meet here at eight."

I nodded and we parted.

12

Sarah and I were on the bus. She sat behind the wheel. She turned the key and the bus started up.

I had walked to the bus that morning after having breakfast with my aunt. I was surprised how new it looked as it gleamed in the morning sun.

It was mostly a very soft blue with a white V-shaped font design on the front. The side windows were small, but the windshield was very wide.

A possum had jumped out the front door when I first reached the bus, but then it ran off. I hesitated to get in behind the wheel so I looked in the back at first but there was nothing there so I sat behind the wheel. That night I was going to fulfill a dream which was to drive away with Sarah. Now we sat side by side in the front seat as she slowly navigated our way over the uneven and bumpy dirt road.

When the engine turned it shook up the silence. I loved making an impact. As we drove down the dirt road the sky wasn't as clear as it was the night before so I couldn't see as much outside through the passenger window.

"There's the quarry," she said.

I could see a large dark empty three-story wooden, brick and steel building looming in the near distance. In minutes we were off the dirt road and now on a deserted but paved road.

"This is the town road. It will lead us to the main road to Saugerties."

I watched Sarah drive. She used the rearview mirror and her side mirror as if she had driven every day.

"My father taught me on his Chevy when I was only eleven," she said as if reading my mind.

I watched as she took us safely passed the tall trees and small shrubs that lined each side.

"A deer!" she shouted.

I saw the deer waiting on the side of the road as we passed.

"There's the main road," she said.

She easily turned right, accelerated and we were on our way.

*

I suppose I should have known that our trip was for her to meet up with Billy Dean and no other reason. She didn't even mention his name but when we pulled up to the bowling alley before I could even ask her why we were there, I knew.

We did little talking on our road trip. Mainly when we did speak it was about her desire to see the world.

Most of the trip I thought about us being a married couple and how unlike my parents we were doing everything together and getting along so well we would be inseparable.

Sarah parked the car in the lot where the other kids were hanging out and right in the center of everything was Billy Dean looking like a movie star.

Sarah was flustered. She jumped out from behind the wheel and rushed over to him. In fact, she was hugging him with her hands around his waist before I even got out of the bus.

"Cool wheels," someone said to me, but I ignored them. I inched over to Sarah and Billy Dean. He shot me a look, but it was without malice. When I reached them, Sarah turned to me.

"Billy Dean got drafted," she said.

Burbalack appeared with two bottles of beer handing one to Billy Dean.

"The chick can't have any," Burbalack said referring to Sarah.

"They got me, little guy," Billy Dean said.

I felt significant that he was sharing something of monumental importance to him with me. I felt my chest puff up and my shoulders grow another couple of inches.

"It's a major drag," Burbalack said.

I realized then that Billy Dean had been holding court dispensing his news to the kids of Saugerties. He did look overwhelmed with worry, which is something I had noticed at the police station. He was paler than usual, and his gait was less confident. Even his perfectly coifed hair looked stilted by frayed nerves.

"I already did my physical and took their literacy test but not in a million years did I think they would call me," Billy Dean said.

"What am I going to do without you, man?" Burbalack sighed.

They hugged. It was a strange hug. Burbalack was holding Billy Dean tightly and Billy Dean was trying to sneak out of the hug.

All the while Buralack was eying Sarah. I noticed he was looking at her differently now. There was an odd stare he was using, an intense interest, a vacuous glare that made me uneasy.

"He goes in tomorrow at the crack of dawn," Burbalack said to Sarah. "He has to be there before seven a.m. or they lock him up."

"I know," she countered. Clearly, she wanted him to know that his attempt at upping her with his "inside" information failed.

"So, I stay out all night and report first thing in the morning," Billy Dean announced.

"You'll have plenty of time to sleep in boot camp," someone said.

"Bullshit," Burbalack stated. "You get no sleep in boot camp. They wake you before dawn and you only sleep when you collapse. So, I heard."

I thought I could see Billy Dean already collapsing. For the first time that summer he looked fragile to me, and I wondered if he would survive the rigors of boot camp.

We spent the entire day in front of the bowling alley with the occasional jaunt to the diner. That night a Sheriff's Department car showed up. But when the sheriff's deputy confronted Burbalack and Billy Dean, and he learned about Billy Dean being drafted, I could see him react physically.

"Too bad," he said, meaning it. "I got a cousin in Boston who got drafted. On his first day there he told my uncle that the guys in his platoon were so scared they were all trying to figure out ways of being sent home. One guy went as far as cutting up his own trigger finger. Another guy shot himself in the foot with his M16."

Billy Dean's eyes bulged out and he took a deep slug of his bottled beer.

"Don't shoot your foot off, man," Burbalack said.

"The only way out is if you are married and you have a kid," the deputy sheriff said.

"That ain't going to happen," Burbalack said.

"Look, Billy Dean, get drunk, stay out all night. I won't bother you guys anymore if you promise me not to start any fights or anything," the deputy sheriff said.

"Promise," Burbalack said.

The deputy sheriff stepped up to Billy Dean. "Come back in one piece, kid. No body bag for you, promise?"

Billy Dean nodded. He was so scared he could hardly speak.

"Maybe the war won't last too long," Sarah said. "Maybe by the time Billy Dean gets there it will be over."

"Sorry but that won't happen," the deputy sheriff said. "President Johnson wants to show the Commies that we mean business. This war is just heating up."

Then the deputy sheriff turned to me. "Kid, hopefully this war is over before *you* get drafted."

The thought that I would be in Billy Dean's shoes someday in the future ripped through my sense of security like the hollowing winds of a hurricane. I was momentarily stunned. I even saw how Sarah looked at me with an enormous sense of pity when she realized I had a comradery with Billy Dean. It was like he and I shared something in common. We were young men, or I was about to be in a few more years, and war was coming for us. It already got him and someday it might call to me.

What I wondered was why Burbalack had not been drafted? But it seemed that no one there was asking that question now.

On his way back to his patrol car the deputy sheriff stopped in front of the VW bus. He looked back at us for a moment.

Billy Dean shrugged his shoulders, and the deputy sheriff wrote out a ticket and placed it on the windshield.

"Your registration expired," Billy Dean said. "I noticed when you drove up. You're also missing a sticker on your plates, but he didn't see that."

"It's not ours," Sarah said.

"We stole it," I said and for the first time in my life I felt cool.

"Nice," Billy Dean said.

It was an empowering feeling. It was as if everything about me was suddenly cool. My hair style, my clothes, my sneakers. It was as if I belonged hanging out with Billy Dean, Burbalack and the rest of the older teens.

Even though nothing about me was cool, not my hair style, not my clothes nor my sneakers. I didn't belong with Billy Dean, Burbalack and the rest of the teens. But the truth was that the VW bus was not mine nor Sarah's so it was stolen and we were desperados.

"You are desperadoes, you two," Burbalack said.

The rest of the night I felt I truly belonged in that cool crowd in the bowling alley parking lot in nowhere Saugerties in the late summer of 1965.

*

It was somewhere near four a.m. when Burbalack told Billy Dean that they should start driving to Albany to the recruitment center where Billy Dean would have to report. Billy Dean was so drunk he could hardly stand. As petite as she was Sarah was holding him up from one side as Burbalack occasionally threw his arms around Billy Dean.

In a flash Billy Dean walked away from them both and trembled; and then he sobbed. He sobbed like a first grader. He sobbed like an infant overwhelmed with the complexity of things he could not comprehend and the only way to vent his frustration was to wail.

His sobbing mortified everyone including Sarah. She drifted away from him.

"Let it out, man," Burbalack said loudly.

Sarah drifted towards me. I took her hand. She held it.

"He's upset," she said.

"I never saw anybody cry like that," I said.

"Me neither."

Burbalack again threw his arms around Billy Dean and it had a sobering effect. Billy Dean pushed him away, pulled his dungaree jacket towards his chest.

"I'll man up here."

"You are a man," Burbalack said.

"Okay, people. I'm off," Billy Dean said then turned without any more fanfare and staggered to Burbalack's pickup truck.

Sarah watched it all when she suddenly bolted from my side, raced to Billy Dean and put her arms around him.

He raised his head and looked up at the slowly turning night sky. It was no longer without light. It was slowly turning a deep purple.

His body went limp, with his arms at his side, looking as if he were about to take off and fly away. Sarah buried her head in his chest for a long time until Billy Dean pulled himself away and got into the passenger side.

Burbalack followed, got in behind the wheel, and started up the pickup.

Sarah didn't move. The few other teens left in the parking lot who had gathered were motionless zombies. They neither spoke nor waved.

As Burbalack spun the pickup around Billy Dean leaned his head out of the window and faced us but he didn't look at us. He looked *through* us. I can still see his wavy soft blond hair frozen into place by hair gel and his pale complexion and large lips frozen in time.

I can still see his bleary, red-eyed stare as he investigated his dark future. I wondered if he was starting that thing people do as they struggle to control their emotions. I wonder if he was already accepting the inevitable allowing his being to become a passive vessel as he started his journey into the frightening unknown.

In moments, the pickup disappeared into the town lights and beyond.

"I should have gone with him," Sarah said.

I took her hand again and led her to the VW bus.

"I can't drive," I told her embarrassed by my announcement since I had plans of driving us across country.

Sarah didn't seem to care. She got behind the wheel and drove us out of town and without incident back to the deserted narrow road which led to the dirt road and the rock quarry.

"He won't die in Vietnam, will he?"

"I don't think everybody who goes to fight there dies otherwise they wouldn't be sending soldiers to fight, right?"

"Yes," she said turning to me.

"Billy Dean is tough."

"He's not."

I didn't say anything to her when I heard her say that.

When we reached the rock quarry she parked the VW bus. I noticed the ticket on the windshield.

"Should we leave it?"

She took it off the windshield and threw it away.

We got out and walked back to the cornfield.

I walked her home. The purple sky was now turning a dark blue. She held my hand.

When we reached her house, we hid behind the stalks of corn. Her house was dark.

"I'll slip in. They won't even know I was gone."

"This was a big night," I said.

"Yeah. It was."

She kissed me on the lips. I felt a shock race through my nerves.

She pressed her lips against mine. I wasn't sure what I was supposed to do so I didn't do anything.

She then buried her face in my neck and left it there. I put both arms around her.

"You are special to me," she said.

"I love you," I muttered.

She kissed my cheek and put her hand in my hair. She then turned and walked to her house. I watched her go in through the back entrance.

I then turned and walked through the cornfield as the sun reached the horizon. When I reached the porch, my aunt was still there in the bright porch light. I tiptoed passed her hoping the noisy screen door wouldn't wake her and it didn't.

I then walked past the den where my uncle slept soundly to the sound of pop music.

The big clock rang five times. I walked upstairs to my room, got undressed and got into bed.

I was facing west so I was fortunate that the sun wouldn't bathe my room until late afternoon.

13

Sarah's curfew was lifted as the dog days of summer slowly ran down. She was allowed out at night and the first thing she did was turn the VW bus into our *hang out*. She managed to find old blankets, pillows, candles and bed sheets and she brought them to the bus and decorated it like a trailer.

We took out the back seats and placed the blankets and pillows side by side so we could hang out together and talk. She also found some paint around her house, so we painted peace symbols and sayings like, *Live and Love* on the side of the bus with white paint.

Sarah was very expressive and creative with some other designs. She painted a large star on the blue VW bus and painted little stick figures with smiling faces looking up at the bright sun.

"I want all people to be happy," she said.

At night it got chilly as August moved along and she would wear this pretty blue sweater.

One day when I was wearing my dungaree jacket, we exchanged them and soon I was wearing her sweater and going home in it, and she was wearing my jacket.

One night my aunt noticed.

"I got it from Sarah," I told her.

"So, you two are becoming an item."

I didn't respond but the next night at dinner my uncle took me into the den.

"We need to have a talk," he said.

"About what?"

"Did your father ever tell you about the birds and the bees?"

"Sure," I lied.

I wasn't exactly sure what the birds and the bees had to do with my feelings for Sarah other than I was totally in the dark about what I was supposed to do other than kiss her.

I knew she liked being kissed and I did like feeling her hands on my face, running through my hair and wrapped about my shoulders but that was the extent of what we did.

"Well, ya see, when a boy likes a girl certain things happen to them. It's biological. Has anything like that happened to you and this Viola girl yet?"

"I don't think so."

My uncle looked confused. "Okay, so the problem is you don't want to get a girl pregnant. Not at your age. And I certainly don't want you to ruin your young life while you were living with your aunt and me."

"I won't ruin my life."

He looked relieved.

"Good to hear. Now if you have any questions, you come right to me and your aunt. You got that?"

"Yes."

That was the end of our conversation.

*

Sarah and I did have our own conversation.

One night she had asked me if she could tattoo me with her name on my belly. I told her it was okay. So, I pulled up my shirt and let her be creative. She wrote her name with flair with a blue pen above my belly button. It was titillating feeling the pen and watching her intently looking at my bare chest and belly.

When she was done, she kissed my belly button.

"For good luck," she said. "Now I want you to write your name on me."

"Okay."

She gave me the pen then turned around and got on her left side.

"Write it on my hip," she said as she undid her pants belt and slowly edged her jeans down over her hips.

I felt my heart shudder seeing her naked hip in the dim candlelight. I watched as she gently pulled the tip of her jeans, and even the top half of her white panties, down to the soft curve of her bottom.

I felt a surge of exhilaration. I was also startled and unable to move.

She turned to me. "You still there?"

"Yes," I murmured.

"Draw *Chris* nice."

"I'm not as artistic as you. It won't be very good."

"Try."

I slowly leaned in with my blue pen and found an incredibly soft spot on her hip. I could hardly take my eyes off the curvature of her bottom and though she didn't reveal everything to me it was still enough to stop the heartbeat and race up the breathing of a thirteen-year-old boy.

I did my best to print my name pressing down on her derriere and completed my *Chris.*

Sarah then pulled up her pants. "I can check it out in the bathroom mirror when I get home."

She could see how shaky I was.

"You, okay?"

"I saw you naked. No, I'm not okay."

"Sorry."

She pulled me closer. "It was exciting for me, too."

"It was?"

"Oh, yeah."

We kissed and our kissing seemed otherworldly. I felt like my body was elevated, rising slowly up in the VW bus, spinning around in the small space where our two thin, petite bodies were drifting in a world I certainly had never been in before.

I wanted to ask Sarah if she had ever kissed anyone like she had kissed me before, but I thought better of it. I knew how much she had liked Billy Dean so I figured I might not get the answer I wanted to hear.

After we would kiss petrified in our motion like one of the great petrified trees in California, we would untangle and lie back side by side looking up at the sky through the large windshield. We would lie side by side taking in the silence and one another in a perfect universe. All went well like this for a little while until one day Marsha appeared outside the bus.

It was a warm sunny afternoon and we both noticed her sitting outside on a rock a few yards away just facing us without saying anything.

"Marsha's outside," I told Sarah.

We had been playing cards both barefoot with our legs wrapped together in some pretzel that Sarah had devised. It was so odd to be this physically close to a female. I had never been that close to one before and it made me think of my father and mother and it gave me some knowledge of why they had gotten together in the first place. It was the physical attraction between the sexes that brought them together.

Sarah and I put on our sneakers and went outside.

"So, this *is* where you two have been. Everybody wondered. You're playing house together," Marsha said.

"What's up?" Sarah asked.

"The summer's almost over and I was looking to hang with you."

"Oh."

"Don't you want to hang with me?"

"I'm kinda hanging with Chris."

"I see that."

Sarah stepped onto the rock, and I followed. Now all three of us were sitting on the rock. The cicadas made their late summer sounds.

"Wow the crickets got loud," I said.

"City boy is stupid. They are not crickets they're cicadas."

"He's not stupid," Sarah said.

"I think he is."

I wasn't sure how to react. I watched as Sarah stood up and walked back to the bus. "Let's go."

"What, you two are going to hide in there and make out? Like, what, nobody knows what you're doing? You know what your problem is? You're *both* stupid."

Sarah turned again but this time I stepped in front of her.

"Why don't you leave?" I said.

"Make me."

Before Marsha stood, Sarah rushed her. She jumped up onto Marsha as if she were a ladder. Marsha was bigger so in this fight she just stood up, grabbed Sarah's shoulders, and pushed her down.

I ran behind Marsha and pulled on her, but she was also bigger than me and with one shove she knocked me back and I fell into the tall grass. Marsha was on top of Sarah in a second and, with her face over Sarah's, she kissed her on the mouth.

I took a long look and saw Marsha rubbing herself against Sarah and Sarah cringing and squirming to get out from under her.

Marsha then stopped. She got up and lifted Sarah up onto her feet. "I love you," she said.

Sarah rubbed the dirt from my jacket that she was wearing. "I don't love you."

"Please, have feelings for me."

"I don't have any feelings for you."

Marsha turned pale. It was as if I wasn't even there and, in fact, I felt left out of this oddly enthusiastic and turbulent interaction.

Marsha shook her head and threw herself against the bus. "You love him?" she asked without even gesturing to me.

"I don't love *you*, that's for sure."

Marsha now turned to me. "Tell her how much I care about her."

I smirked. I wasn't sure why. But I did. The entire episode was absurd to me and oddly adult. There was nothing innocent about it at all. It was scary in that way.

Marsha moved to Sarah to hug her, and this time Sarah pushed her away. "Get out of here!"

"I can't."

"We are friends, Marsha. And that's all."

I thought how this personal and secretive, emotional display seemed surreal in the bright sunshine.

"I can't just be friends with you."

"I'm sorry but that's how I feel."

Marsha sighed. She lowered her head and made a guttural sound. She then turned her back to us and walked away.

Sarah and I both watched Marsha walk towards the cornfield and vanish into the now yellow stalks. Sarah went back into the bus, and

I followed. Once inside, she found a towel and wiped away the dirt from her face. I saw a rash on her neck.

"You're red there."

"Thanks," she said, then buried her face in my chest.

I felt for the first time in my life what a man does when a woman needs comfort from him. I said nothing, allowing her to feel that very comfort. Sarah didn't cry. In fact, she was resolute.

"I didn't mean to hurt her but I always knew she had a crush on me. Remember when I told you? It started last summer. How she always wanted to be alone with me. I thought it was because she just wanted to be friends, but she got jealous of you this time." We then both laid down on the blanket and spent the rest of the afternoon quietly holding one another, gently kissing and allowing the afternoon to become as quiet as we were inside. Though it was warm the bus stayed oddly cool, or we didn't feel the August heat being that close to one another.

It was that time in August when the sunlight grew heavier, and the sun set earlier. I watched the light go from white to a deeper yellow.

14

That night my aunt and uncle huddled in front of the TV. I could see Black people running through the streets breaking into stores. They called it looting.

"What happened?"

"Riots."

"Where?" I asked.

"Los Angeles," my aunt said. "California."

"Where the Dodgers play?"

"Yeah," my uncle said.

"Watts. It's in Los Angles," my aunt said.

"Crazy how they destroy the stores where they live," my uncle said.

"Why are they doing that?"

All three of us were watching the fuzzy black and white images of angry young people breaking windows and police officers, with batons, hitting them.

"They're angry," my uncle said.

"How come?"

"A cop shot one of them dead," my aunt said.

"Why are only Black people rioting?"

"Because they don't have jobs," my uncle said.

"And they came here as slaves," my aunt said.

That notion perplexed me. "They came here as slaves?"

"They were sold down south to pick cotton," my uncle said.

"Down south?"

"Alabama and Mississippi," my aunt said.

I watched TV sets and stereos carried through the streets. I thought I saw the police hose looters and rioters down with water.

"Where are they from?"

"Africa," my uncle told me.

"Who made them slaves?"

"Didn't they teach you anything about the Civil War in school?" my aunt asked.

"I guess. The Blue and the Gray."

"It was more than that," my aunt said.

I was taught about something called states' rights. This was entirely different.

I walked out of the den and onto the porch. I looked out in the dark and saw how calm it was and how the cornfield and the surrounding woods were so different than what I saw on the TV. The anger and violence were nowhere to be seen.

My aunt followed me with her highball. "Tough to watch that kind of thing right there in your own living room."

"Will that happen here?" I asked.

"It did in Harlem. It can happen anywhere when people don't think they are getting their fair share." She made her way outside the screen door and into the front yard.

I followed and watched her standing under the stars. The stars were everywhere. Off over the hill the crescent moon hung like it was on invisible hooks.

"Life can be hard sometimes. People lose their patience. Sometimes they are very wrong in what they do and sometimes, you can see and understand why they do what they do even if it hurts themselves and other people."

She sipped her highball and turned back to the house. I heard the *Bonanza* theme song play.

"Papa had enough of the news," she said.

I edged closer to her. "Aunt, can a girl like another girl."

"You mean as friends?"

"Well, in a way that she kisses her."

"When did that happen?"

"Today with Sarah and her friend Marsha."

"They kissed in front of you?"

"Not exactly. Marsha kissed Sarah but Sarah didn't want her to."

My aunt mulled it over and took another slug. "When I was just old enough to go to a bar that happened to me once."

"Some girl kissed you?"

"Yes. And she put her hand on my leg."

I felt a sudden sense of being an adult with her sharing this with me.

"I was at the bar with my girlfriends and one of them was with her cousin. Not a girl I knew well. She was from Prospect Park. Pretty girl. Elegant. We had met once before. She was very friendly with me that night. We got along in an instant. She had big brown eyes and a nice smile."

I listened closely.

"Well, I know it's hard to imagine, but I was a pretty girl. I was nineteen, I think. We always went out with skirts and heels and made up our hair and put on lipstick and makeup. Like the way you think that Viola girl is pretty is the way kids my age then thought I was pretty. Your uncle Marty too was a handsome young man. He wasn't always husky like he is now. He had nice brown hair and strong shoulders. Anyway, I didn't know him then but this girl, for the life of me I can't remember her name now. Louise? Laura? Anyway, that night we were all drinking and listening to the music from this band and I thought I had met a particularly good new friend."

"What happened?"

"Hard to say. But what I can tell you is that she put her hand on my leg."

"Why?"

"For a lot of reasons. She was sitting next to me at the bar. We had been dancing together and talking about boys, so I didn't think nothing of it at first. But then when we were ready to go home, she kissed me."

"On the lips?"

"On the lips. I was okay with it at first since that was the way girls were with one another in those days. Friendly, touchy, and warm. But then she kissed me again and this time I knew what the kiss was about. I had never kissed anybody boy or girl like that before."

"Did she say anything?"

"She did. 'I didn't know I would do that,' is what she said."

My aunt pushed her glass to the side of her face. "Warm night."

"Yes. What happened then?"

I could see the glass sweating in the harsh light from the porch. My aunt looked younger, standing there in her light blue and white house dress and her brown slippers.

"I told her I wasn't like that. She kissed me again and this time I had to be firm."

"Firm?"

"I told her that it was not me. 'That is *not* me,' I said to her."

"Not you?"

"Not a lesbian."

"What's that?"

"A woman who likes women, in that way. They have other harsher words for it but I would never use them."

"Were you scared?"

"No, not scared. I felt sorry for her. She looked up at me with those big eyes. 'I thought I met someone who knew me,' she said. Or something like that."

"Knew you?"

"By that she meant someone who understood her. When I looked at her at that moment, she looked so lonely. It hurt me she looked so sad."

I glanced up at the crescent moon. It was fading behind clouds.

My aunt turned to me. "You made me think about that night. I thought I had forgotten all about it. I haven't thought about it for years. Years!"

She smiled. I smiled back at her.

"All this time has gone by and here I am this night wondering about that lovely young woman, what happened to her and how she managed."

My aunt's voice sounded young, soft. Blissful.

She took another sip from her drink.

"I'm tired, Chris," she said. "The summer is ending. You'll be back in school and starting your life and it will all be grand."

"Why didn't you and Uncle Marty have kids?"

"We couldn't. One of us couldn't and then after a while we didn't care. We have each other."

She walked back to the house, onto the porch and sat down at the table in her spot under the porch light. She sipped her drink a few more times lost in thought, memories, and the odd passage of time.

As I watched her, I wondered if she was still thinking of that lonely young woman as she described her. I also wondered why people remember the things they remember and forget the things they forget? And most of all, I wondered why we remember things at all.

With the harsh light on her face, with the crescent moon and stars gone away, she closed her eyes and fell asleep.

I looked at her aging face with its creases and wrinkles and tried to imagine her young.

*

Sarah and I spent time together for the next few weeks talking about the end of summer and how Labor Day would come and go, the trees would turn yellow and then the snow would come.

"You'll be gone long before all that happens."

"I can come up and visit you and you can come to the city and visit me," I told her.

The days were getting shorter, and we spent most of our time talking about our futures. When you're young the future means that coming week. I had a tough time imagining anything more. Sometimes I could envision graduating grammar school but that was as far as I could imagine. I suppose when you're young, the past is very concrete. It's the future that is a blur.

Also, time stood still when I was with Sarah. The day moved slowly. The sun hung still in the sky all day. When night came, it was the moon that hardly moved. When I was with Sarah the night sky grew bigger, the moon more luminous and the stars were not so distant.

We kissed a lot, and the more we kissed the more those physical feelings were aroused in me. I had no idea what to do about them.

"Do you believe in the moon?"

"Yes," I told her.

I was a virgin and so was Sarah. I was sure I knew what it meant to be a virgin and I knew I was going to remain one but I was not sure what it meant *not* to be a virgin.

"I want to see my name," I said. I had asked Sarah this several times, and every time I did, she obliged. She would get on her side and pull down her jeans and panties just enough over her hips for me to see *Chris*.

"You like this, don't you?"

"I do," I told her. "Can I feel it a little?"

"Yes, you can," she said.

And then I would touch her gently on her hip excited by what I felt, but even more by what I *saw*. I was very aware that I was moving into unchartered territory. I was moving into a place of unknown emotions and physical excitement all without a road map or any knowledge of the terrain.

The thought that anyone else would ever see Sarah's hip, as I was seeing it then in the soft afternoon light in that cramped but ideal VW bus, angered me.

"I don't want my name to ever wash off."

"When I shower, I try not to let the water run there."

"Does your mother watch you in the shower?"

"Of course not."

"Good. I don't want anyone to ever see my name but me."

"For how long?"

"Months. Years."

Sarah gave me a slight smile.

All was paradise until Burbalack's pickup showed up in Sarah's front yard one morning. I could see Sarah and Burbalack talking to one another then I watched them walk into the cornfield.I quickly finished my breakfast and waited on my side of the cornfield.

Eventually they appeared, walking side by side toward me. I had a premonition that startled me. It was a vision of something that had already happened or it was a foreshadowing of something that was going to happen.

"Mike got a letter from Billy Dean," Sarah said. "We're going to read it in the bus."

Burbalack hadn't changed. He was still tall and lanky, and his black hair was combed back. He was wearing a short-sleeved red plaid shirt, jeans and boots. I thought how one day I would be wearing that same outfit someday.

"Hey," he said.

"Hey," I said back. I noticed that he was more subdued than I had ever seen him.

Once we walked to the bus, we sat outside leaning against it and Burbalack handed Sarah the letter.

"You never opened it," she said.

Burbalack remained silent.

Sarah looked at me, then opened the letter. "Mike," she read. "It's for you. You read it."

She handed him the letter. He reluctantly took it. But he just held it.

"You want to read it alone?" she asked.

He looked away.

"I can't read."

I was confused. I wondered if he meant he couldn't read it because it would upset him or that he didn't want to read it.

"What do you mean?" Sarah asked.

"I never learned to read," he said.

He slid down the side of the bus. He was sitting next to Sarah. I was sitting with my legs crossed facing them both. He handed Sarah the letter.

"It was why I wasn't drafted with Billy Dean. I'm 4F."

Sarah opened the letter. She looked up. We were in the shade from a tall tree so the late August air was cool. The wind was picking up, but it was still gentle, as I remember Sarah's eyes to be at that moment.

"Mike, hope all is good with you. Write me, man. Boot camp is hell down here at Fort Dix. But I got my dog tags and my M1 and my combat boots. They say we are all going to Nam. The only weird thing is that they train us in hills and mountains, but

Nam is all jungle. We got no jungle here in the states to train so we have to figure it out when we get there. Come down and visit me, man. On my last day I get a 24-hour pass. Then they fly us to Asia. Billy Dean. P.S. I know you will need someone to read this to you. Who cares you can't read? No big deal. Anyway, it kept you out of the Army!"

Sarah lowered the letter.

"Where's Fort Dix?"

"Jersey," Burbalack said. "I'm going. Can you write him back for me to tell him I'm going?"

"I can, yes," Sarah said.

We sat in silence.

"I'm scared for him," Sarah said.

"The war is heating up, you know," Burbalack said.

Eventually Burbalack got up and Sarah and I walked him back to his pickup.

When we got there, he took out a cigarette and lit it up. "Do me a favor and don't tell anybody about me not being able to read."

I nodded.

Burbalack walked away.

"When are you going?" Sarah asked.

"His last day is next week. Labor Day." He got into his pickup and drove away.

Sarah drifted back into the cornfield and found a shady spot and sat. I sat next to her.

"What's wrong?"

"Life sucks."

"Not all the time."

"How come everything is so hard?"

"I don't know," I said.

"I don't believe in sin or heaven and hell. But sometimes I wish there was a heaven so that all this is worth it, you know?"

"I know."

I'm not sure how long we sat there but the sun set and mosquitoes started to buzz around us.

"I better get home," Sarah said.

I walked her back to her door. She kissed me on the cheek and went back inside.

I walked back through the cornfield and when I got home my aunt and uncle were already sitting at the dinner table.

I saw the plate of bread and the bowl of boiled carrots and the pork chops and the glasses of water alongside by aunt's highball.

"What's wrong?" she asked.

"Billy Dean is going to be sent to Vietnam probably."

"It's what men do, they go to war," my uncle said taking a bite out of his corn on the cob.

I had little appetite. That night I walked to the bus, but Sarah never showed up. I walked to the edge of the cornfield and saw that her light was on. I was worried that something had happened to her but decided to go home and check in on her the following morning.

The following morning, I knocked on her door but nobody answered. I saw her mother's car was gone.

I spent all day in the bus by myself fighting a tremendous sense of unseen catastrophe though I had no idea what was causing the feeling. When I got home, my aunt was waiting for me.

"Your father called. He's coming to pick you up at the end of the week. He wants you home for Labor Day weekend. School starts for you that Tuesday."

The sense of catastrophe was crystalizing and morphing into a tangible entity. My leaving, Billy Dean's going off to war, and Sarah's mystifying absence.

The next morning at dawn, I was at Sarah's house knocking on the door.

Her mother appeared with blurry eyes. "Sarah's not here."

"Huh?"

"She left yesterday to see her father," she said.

"Her father?"

"Didn't she tell you?"

"No."

"Oh."

I felt so close to Sarah being at her door I nearly asked her mother if I could wait for her in her room. I had never seen her room, but I had imagined it so many times.

"When is she coming back?"

"She has to come back to go to school."

"Can I call her?"

Sarah's mother gave me a long look. "Let me check. I'll call your aunt and let you know." She closed the door.

I couldn't move. My heart was shattered and yet the feeling was so alien to me I didn't exactly know what to do. I had never had a broken heart before. It took me a few moments to become aware of my surroundings and walk back to the house.

For the next few days, I avoided the bus. I roamed the pathways through the woods around Sarah's house hoping to see her back home. I moped around the creek where we first kissed, and then back to the quarry. I walked passed the VW bus trying not to get too close, afraid I'd be contaminated by the poison of lost love. I had no idea why she didn't tell me she was leaving. I had no idea why she didn't explain to me about seeing her father.

I saw her face everywhere I walked. When I sat in my room, I imagined her there as if she was in the beginning of the summer when I hid her and gave her money to see Billy Dean. At one time, I did enter the VW bus telling myself that she would return and I should clean it and have it ready for her. I laid down where I did, imagining she was there, and talked to her as if she were. But the following day I woke up angry at breakfast, being short with my aunt and uncle.

"Where is the Viola girl?" my aunt asked.

"With her father," I said. "Did her mother call?"

"Nobody called, Chris."

Then I left the house and paced back and forth in the backyard with Stalin's barking my only company.

My father eventually came to pick me up. It was a humid morning with rain in the forecast. I was packed and ready to go.

My aunt hugged me. My uncle, who had been working in the shack joined us at the car with Stalin in tow.

I hardly acknowledged my father who held my suitcase. My aunt took him aside and I overheard her explain why I was sulking.

She gave me a heartfelt hug.

"I loved having you here, Christopher. It meant a lot to me and your uncle."

"Thank them for taking care of you," my father told me.

"Thanks," I said.

"Don't let the little girl get to you," my uncle said to me.

"Oh, be quiet, Papa," my aunt said.

"What did I say?" my uncle asked, looking oddly perplexed.

As my father's car made the long turn up toward the mushroom farm, I looked back and saw my aunt and uncle standing in the front yard watching me go. They looked so lonely, and the house so isolated, I was suddenly struck by the fact that I had spent an entire summer there and I wondered how that was possible.

It started to rain. My uncle turned and led Stalin back to his doghouse, but my aunt stood in the rain for a few moments watching me go. I then watched her rush away and into the house.

My father put on the windshield wipers, took the car over the hill and through the trees, and down the road towards Sarah's house. I sat next to him feeling a sudden nostalgia for a place I had not even left yet.

I didn't want to talk about my mother or anything else. I was unable to think about tomorrow or the day after.

But I was young and if I was going to have my heart broken, I needed to accept that it was only the beginning of the long passage into adulthood. I no doubt would have my heart broken many more times.

I looked at Sarah's house as we drove passed.

"Your aunt said that's the girl's house. Do you want to stop and see her before we go?"

"No sense in doing that."

"Why not?"

"She's not there," I said, then faced the road and settled in for the long trip home.

THE END

About the Author

RICHARD VETERE's teleplay adaptation of his published stage play *The Marriage Fool*, starring Walter Matthau, Carol Burnett and John Stamos, is now streaming on Amazon. His novel *The Writers Afterlife*, published in 2014, was called "a unique caper of magic realism" by Publishers Weekly. His new play *Zaglada*, was published by Dramatic Publishing in 2019. His screenplay *Caravaggio*, an adaptation of his own published stage play, won the Golden Palm Award for Best Screenplay at the Beverly Hills International Film Festival in 2021. His *Live Fast, Die Young & Leave a Good-Looking Corpse: a memoir of the 1970s* was published in 2021. He co-wrote the movie *The Third Miracle*, which is a screenplay adaptation of his own novel, published by Simon & Schuster. It was produced by Francis Ford Coppola, directed by Agnieszka Holland, and stars Ed Harris and Anne Heche. He has a master's degree in Comparative English Literature from Columbia University and has lectured on screenwriting and playwrighting in the master's program at NYU and lectures now at Queens College. In 2005, the Frank Melville Library at Stony Brook University created the Richard Vetere Collection, an archive of his work. RichardVetereauthor.com

PAOLO A. GIORDANO, Ed. *Joseph Tusiani: Poet. Translator. Humanist.*
  Vol 2. Criticism.
ROBERT VISCUSI. *Oration Upon the Most Recent Death of Christopher Columbus.*
  Vol 1. Poetry.